A Simple Twist of Fate

Also by Antonia Hildebrand and published by Ginninderra Press
The Blind Colossus
To Breathe & other stories
War Stories: Poems for the Age of Fallibility

Antonia Hildebrand

A Simple Twist of Fate
& other stories

A Simple Twist of Fate
ISBN 978 1 76041 939 4
Copyright © text 2020
Cover design: Mary Ann Hine

First published 2020 by
GINNINDERRA PRESS
PO Box 3461 Port Adelaide 5015
www.ginninderrapress.com.au

Contents

A Simple Twist of Fate	7
Cold	17
King Crab	25
Modern Love	29
Musical Chairs	40
Pretenders	50
Straight	56
Stump	65
True North	76
The Eye Out of a Needle	84
Rome, Twice	96
A Delirium	111
The Pointy End	120

A Simple Twist of Fate

The first time I saw her, she was in a broken-down car. I'm not big on metaphors but this was one. Her life up to that point had been a broken-down car and I had come along and found her in it. I got the car going again and she was so grateful she was close to tears. She was a tall, willowy blonde with blue-grey eyes. I thought she was very beautiful. Easy to describe but impossible to define. What defined her most was absence. An absence of confidence, an absence of balance – those were her hallmarks. And what came with them was a neediness so vast that I had nothing to compare it to until we took a trip to the Blue Mountains and I saw Govett's Leap.

That was the scale of her neediness – it was as vast and primeval as that landscape and like Govett's Leap it spread in all directions. Nothing touched her insecurity: not her beauty, not her brains and not her success as a financial planner. She was jealous and possessive and needed constant reassurance. In bed, she was a volcano – all slow heat and unpredictability. Not quite insatiable but driven by uncontrolled need, as she was out of bed. Even her name was ambiguous: Edwina – 'But everyone calls me Eddie.'

Once we became a couple, she called me 'honey', only rarely by my name. She didn't much like my name, which was Gerard. I didn't much like it either.

She was so highly strung that if I touched her while she was eating, she would say, 'Don't play with me, honey, or I can't eat.' Playing with her ranged from giving her a peck on the cheek to putting my hand on her leg or her breast.

Her quirkiness and passionate nature were things I found endearing at first. But they hinted at something wayward, something subterranean. Something I didn't know about. I had no idea what.

She had a diary. She wrote in it every day. I wanted to read it, of course, but it was kept in the locked drawer of her desk. There was no way to break into it without leaving evidence. I was sure all the information I needed to understand her was in there but unless I could get the key and open the drawer, the information was out of reach. I told myself that one day I would get the key, copy it and read her diary at my leisure when she was out of the house. But that would not be easy. The key was on a key ring that was always in her handbag, and her handbag was usually with her. I formulated various plans for getting the key but I wasn't obsessed with it. That came later.

I got lucky. She took up jogging and would disappear on early morning runs. She never took her handbag. This made getting the key to her desk drawer ridiculously easy but like many seekers after truth I was plunged into chaos by what I found. I was totally unprepared for what was in that diary of hers. Some of it read like notes for a novel but the dates and the rawness of what it described meant there was no way it could be mistaken for fiction. The distress and the hate were visceral and not confected. The events she described had that quality that is often found in oral histories. However bizarre the events described, they ring true as only lived experiences can. The entry that really caught my eye was this:

10 October 2015

I certainly don't look like a woman who bludgeoned a man to death with a mallet as he lay in bed in our home in June 2014. I know all about domestic violence: I've seen it and I've dealt with it. But that didn't prevent me from becoming trapped and isolated and I couldn't talk about it. People really have to understand no matter how intelligent, no matter how independent you are, it's difficult to come out and ask for help. It's all about visible charm, invisible abuse. No one suspected he was an abuser and no one suspected that I was abused. We both went to great lengths to hide it. And because he was a doctor, no one could imagine he could be violent.

She certainly didn't look, to me, like a woman who was beaten by her husband with a wooden rolling pin and a metal chair, forced to perform sex acts for strangers on Skype and who lived in constant fear of the man who she thought loved her. And yet this is what she described in her diary. It was horrifying and surreal to read but it was so full of both fear and love that I knew it was real. I read on in a frenzy of apprehension. She could come back at any moment and who knew what she would say or do if she caught me reading her diary. Especially given the contents. I had no idea if she had been prosecuted for killing this man, her husband. Soon I decided I had to put it back in the drawer, lock it up and put the key back on the key ring. I placed the diary exactly as I had found it – at least, I hoped I had.

Not much later, she was suddenly there, glowing with sweat. 'I need a shower,' she said, cheerfully, heading up the hall in her pink tracksuit, her blonde ponytail bobbing as she strode along. She looked like the girl next door.

Next time she went jogging, I opened the diary at random and read something that made her situation with this man plain. She was virtually his prisoner even though she was working, earning a good salary and respected in her job and in her life generally.

17 January 2014

Whenever he persuades me to wear something too tight, too short and just too much, he always says, 'Don't worry. They're just jealous,' when people stare and make cruel comments.

He made me wear a very short black skirt to a funeral once. The skirt barely covered the garters I had on my stockings. I could see the looks people were giving me and hear their disgusted comments. I was ashamed.

'They're just jealous,' he said. 'They all wish they looked like you.'

I want to be sexy for him. It's a trap. It obsesses me and he stokes my inferiority complex every chance he gets – little comments that cut like knives – if I don't comply with his demands.

She had plastic surgery on her breasts (twice) because he wanted her to. Enlargements. And his reaction to seeing her breasts carved up, black and blue and with black stitches around the nipples was simply not normal. It excited him and aroused him sexually.

5 June 2013

He came into the recovery room and sat on a chair. He held my hand. He was in such a state of excitement and he persuaded me to unwrap the bandages, even though I wasn't supposed to, and show him my bruised, swollen breasts and the ugly black stitches they put in them. This excites him terribly. That he has such power over me, that I will mutilate my breasts – for him – confirms that I am his creature and can't deny him anything. He wants to climb into the bed with me in the recovery room and have sex with me, regardless of how much pain it will cause me or how much it will affect my recovery. I managed to persuade him that it was a crazy idea and he helped me rewrap my breasts. I looked appalling. My skin was greenish, my lips flaky and dry from hours under anaesthetic. Why would anyone want to have sex with someone who looks like this? Because, I realised later, I have obeyed him, I have suffered and been cut because he has such power over me. This surgery means my breasts are no longer mine, but his. His property. He paid for the surgery.

I only just get the diary back into the drawer and lock it when I hear her opening the front door. I still have to get the key back into her handbag and on the key ring. I do this while she is taking her shower.

Further reading of the diary on other days enhanced the picture I had of their relationship, of their marriage and the torment he inflicted on her.

22 July 2013

Once we were at the beach on a doomed mission to reignite our love. I went to sleep on the beach and got sunburned. He had disappeared and when he came back he was furious.

'Where is he?' he shouted. 'The guy you were talking to, where is he?'

I explain that I have been asleep and not talking to anyone.

'I saw you talking to a man!' he says.

'No, I wasn't. I was asleep,' I say, calmly. Then I walk off down the beach, as fast as I can.

He follows babbling about this man I was supposed to have been talking to. I ignore him and keep walking.

Eventually. he apologises. Says he won't do it again. I accept his apology. He's crazy and his case is hopeless. I'm in a state of despair. I just want him to love me the way I love him but it's not possible for him to do that and I have come to believe that he wants to kill me to end his own torment.

Back at the motel. he is lying on the bed. 'Come here,' he says, patting the space beside him. He is smiling. Charming. The way he can be when it suits him. He is fit and tanned. He is handsome and has bulging biceps. He is very tempting. Above all, he is familiar. A known quantity.

The trip to the beach was meant to rev up our love, such as it was. However, it became a chance for him to criticise me constantly. I had cellulite. I ate too much. Or not enough. I didn't pay him enough attention. Or I paid him too much attention and annoyed him. But I still curl up against his body as if it's where I belong.

Even breaking her leg brought her no respite from his sex mania.

30 July 2013

When I break my leg skiing, he is once more at my side in the recovery room after surgery. For some reason, seeing me helpless or injured causes him to become sexually aroused. My leg is encased in a cast that goes almost to my fork. He holds off until I'm in my hospital bed and then his manic state becomes obvious. He kisses me. My neck is covered in gentle little kisses as he moves upwards towards my mouth. He kisses my lips and slips his tongue in. Then he lies beside me on the hospital bed puts his hands up my shirt, fondles my breasts. At my insistence, he gives me a painkiller and then climbs back on the bed and has sex with me.

The painkiller makes it bearable – but only just. Every movement he makes seems to jolt my body and sends pain coursing through my leg. His selfishness and lack of empathy are incredible. Or would be if I hadn't seen it all before.

The last time, I barely got the diary back into the drawer before she appeared in the hall, looking noticeably slimmer now, even though she had been slender before and didn't need to lose weight – but she was gleaming with health, so I wasn't concerned.

She wanted sex and came up to me, sweaty and beautiful, pressed herself against me and said with a dazzling smile, 'Come and have a shower with me.'

'You start it running,' I told her, because I still had to get the key back into her handbag and on to the key ring. I was playing a dangerous game.

I joined her in the shower and she was playful and sweet and a vision of loveliness. I made love to her and she came with her mouth locked on mine, her body covered in suds. I held her in my arms as she gasped with pleasure.

'Oh, honey,' she purred, kissing my chest, my belly, my neck, my hands. How could she possibly be a murderess? How could any of it be true?

30 May 2014

I had a conversation with my sister on the phone. 'He hit me,' I told her. 'He hit me. He's so cruel sometimes.'

She asks me if I'm okay and I tell her he hit me in the face and on the body and I think my nose and a couple of my ribs might be broken.

She asks me if I'm leaving him and I say no. Then she says, 'Are you going to wait until he kills you?'

After the phone call, there is the humiliating trip to the hospital, on my own, to get medical attention. They try to get me to say I had been beaten but I insist that I had fallen down a flight of stairs. There was no police report, no admission on my part that a crime had occurred – to them or to myself.

10 June 2014

When I expressed my anger at being controlled, his response was to punch my upper arm with a closed fist, as hard as he could. It was very painful and left a bruise that didn't go for a week.

Like a fool, I said, 'Why did you do that? That really hurt.'

He didn't answer. Just stared at me for a while, then walked away.

Two days later, we were arguing over something minor, like whether or not to go shopping, when he suddenly spat in my face.

'What are you doing? Are you crazy?' I said.

He didn't respond with violence. He just gave me a look of contempt and barged out of the room. Then he came back and stood staring at me. 'Get it through your head. You're mine,' he said. 'You'll always be mine.'

'I'm not,' I said in a voice so soft it was little more than a whisper.

He squeezed my arms until the pain was unbearable. Then he pulled me on to the bed, pulled my pants down and forced himself, painfully, inside me.

The next day, he apologised. This was now the familiar pattern. The apology was meaningless. We both knew he would behave this way again. And he was becoming more violent as time went on. Because I accepted it and didn't leave.

12 June 2014

I was going to a party – one that he couldn't attend. Or so I thought. In fact, he suddenly announced that I wasn't going. I asked why.

'Because I said so,' was all he said.

Later that night after we had sex, he beat me again. Even though I had obeyed. Even though I had not challenged his order. It was becoming impossible to know what would set him off.

Eventually, it was just too much trouble, too traumatic to go out at night. When I got home, I would be kept up all night justifying every man I had spoken to, everything I had done. It was an interrogation that left me lost and exhausted. Nothing satisfied him. Not sex, not love and certainly not the truth.

She seemed to be jogging further and further. Each time she went out now, it took longer and longer for her to come back. It was logical, of course, that she would be jogging further as she got fitter. I was able to read more entries and longer entries than before, but I was still playing with fire.

15 June 2014

'Don't you laugh at me!' This is what he screamed as he dragged me out of the bathroom by my hair. He threw me on the bed, rolled me on to my back, sat on my knees and punched me in the face over and over again. 'You'll be dead before morning,' he threatened.

But in the end, exhaustion from beating me made him pass out next to me on the bed. I knew I had to kill him. The thought made me cry, silently – so that I wouldn't wake him. But I knew that he would kill me if I didn't kill him. The next day, my face ached and was bruised and swollen.

'You're so fucking ugly,' was all he said when he saw me.

My mind was racing. I knew I couldn't use a gun – I didn't have one and didn't know how to use one. A knife was too bloody and too cold. I had no idea what to use and that was the only reason he survived another day.

When she came back from jogging this time, I was so overwhelmed by compassion for her that I couldn't make eye contact. She went off to have her shower completely unaware that I was sick and ashamed of what another man had done to her. The diary was back in the desk and the key was back in her handbag.

20 July 2016

They call it the 'triggering event'. This is something worse than the violent male partner has ever done before. In my case, it was a beating that knocked out a couple of teeth, followed by rape. Fortunately, by sheer luck, they weren't front teeth but that is, of course, beside the point. I was left lying on the floor bleeding from my mouth and my face. The rape was horrible – all rapes are. I had told him I didn't want sex that night, that I felt sick – which was true. That sent him into an uncontrollable rage. Though how uncontrollable his rages were was always debatable. If my sister or a friend came around when he was building up to a rage, he could switch it off and play the affable mine host, only to switch it back on when they left.

The prelude to the rape was him pulling my bra down as I was trying to get up from the floor, exposing my breasts.

'Can I kiss them?' he said in a sneering way.

I was still bleeding. 'I'm not in the mood,' I said in bewilderment. Wrong answer.

'I'll put you in the mood,' he said in an ominous voice, soft and threatening.

He then proceeded to suck and bite my nipples in a way that inflicted pain. I tried to push him away and he punched my breasts and then my face. Shocked and dazed, I tried to run but he tackled me to the floor, tore all my remaining clothes off and raped me as painfully as he could. After telling me he would kill me during the night, he left me lying on the floor completely dehumanised, in pain and crying.

I don't remember much about the rest of the night. At some point, he must have crawled up on to the bed and gone to sleep. Nothing I did remains in my memory but I know without any doubt that I did what they say I did.

Was it self-defence? The law decided it was, after a short trial where I pleaded guilty to manslaughter. I was acquitted. The jury accepted I was acting in self-defence when I beat his skull in with a meat mallet as he slept. When I woke and saw him lying on the blood-soaked pillow, I called an ambulance and the police. Which helped me in court. I did all the right things – except, you could say, for beating his head in. That nightmare was over but living with what I had done was another nightmare. One that will never be over.

So my curiosity was satisfied. Now I knew the story and how it had ended and that was something at least. She knew nothing about me reading her diary and continued to be as odd and charming as ever, calling me 'honey' and being ever ready for lovemaking. If I didn't know what I knew, she would have just about been my ideal partner. But the image of her wielding that mallet never left me and would intrude at moments of intimacy, pulling me to a dark place where I had no wish to be. I stayed with her. In time, I came to love her, but I was careful, very careful, about everything I said and everything I did and when she pounded a steak out flat with the meat mallet before cooking it, I felt nauseous and a little worm of fear wriggled near my heart.

Cold

'It was exquisite – I could feel it all the way down to my toes. He bit my breasts then he grabbed my hair and pulled my head back and started kissing me. Eventually I had this seemingly endless orgasm. In fact, it hadn't stopped when he flipped me over and continued from the back. He was beside himself and he was biting the back of my neck. Then he finished. His hands were trembling, and he was like a rag doll. You could get his head between your hands and do this,' I demonstrated by rolling my head from side to side between my hands, laughing as I did so.

My therapist looked odd and slightly pale. My stream of consciousness diatribe had rattled her.

'Are you all right?' I asked, sympathetically.

'I'm perfectly all right, thank you,' she said. But her voice was a bit unsteady. Maybe she'd started to think that she had wasted her life, sitting there in that tastefully furnished room taking notes, while other people were actually living.

All the time I was talking, I knew that I was showing off – that I had made myself into an exhibitionist and her into a voyeur; but I wanted her to know that even though I was a broken human being, I'd had my moments.

It always started with my father humming that tune. I can't remember the tune. I've blocked it. Usually it was a Saturday, but not always. First he would bath me. My mother had left; he said it was because she was a bad woman. I was seven, so I couldn't argue. I had no idea what was true and what wasn't. Years later when I finally tracked her down, alcohol and cancer of the liver had already killed her.

After he bathed me, he would leave me naked and carry me into the bedroom, where I would spend the night with him in the big bed. He would take his own clothes off too and he would lie down with me and hold me in his arms. I enjoyed this. He was my father, I loved him. When I was eight, it changed. He began putting his hand between my legs and kissing me all over my naked body. By the age of nine, we were having sex or, as I now understand, thanks to my therapist, I was being raped or, to use the popular term, molested.

He was a university lecturer so after sex he read me books to improve my mind. Dickens was a favourite. The sound grounding he gave me in literature is why I was later able to do a master's degree in literature and a double major in English literature in my undergraduate degree. He told me that if I told anyone about our special time together he would go to jail. So of course I told no one. He had a special name for what we did in his bed, too. He called it smooching. A harmless word for something that was harming me every time it happened.

'I told Lee there was no future for us as a couple because I was so damaged,' I told the therapist. 'But I didn't tell him why I was damaged.'

'What did he say to that?'

'He gave a short speech. "I've fathered children and watched them being born," he said. "I've seen the blood, the shit, the milk. I've had the milk squirt all over my face. I've changed shitty nappies. I've had women curse me in childbirth and cover me in blood when I was having sex with them. I've held women down who were so drunk they wanted to do themselves a damage. I've had drunken women vomit down my back while I was trying to kiss them. You don't scare me."'

'Quite a turn of phrase,' said the therapist with a strangely bitter little smile.

'And that's when he told me I needed therapy but not to break up with him because that was just running away and I needed to grow a spine.'

'It sounds as if he cares for you a great deal.'

'He does. It amazes me because I basically think I'm worthless.'

'Tell me about him. How did you meet?'

'We met in a bar. He was different from the start.'

'How?'

'I would go out every weekend to bars, say Friday or Saturday night, and bring a man home. The sex was usually soulless and unsatisfactory but I needed to be touched, to be held, not to be alone. He was different. He showed me that sex could be more than therapy – if you'll pardon the expression – that it could be very pleasurable, even a form of ecstatic communication between a man and a woman. I had never experienced that. All my father gave me was sex, but no love – or nothing most people would recognise as love. I remember after Lee got to know me, after he moved in, he told me once that I was like a fire burning at the side of a frozen lake.'

'Can you explain that to me?'

'He said I was sexually manic and emotionally cold. When he would bring me a cup of coffee or tea, I wouldn't even say thank you and I couldn't say I love you because my father made me say that to him. All my expressions of affection are sexual. And then there was the alcohol. As I got older, by about ten, my father could no longer completely control me. Sometimes I would simply refuse to get in the bed with him. So he would get a shot glass and fill it with sherry or whisky and make me drink it. When I was sozzled, he would put me in the bed and rape me. Of course as a teenager I was constantly drunk and running wild. Alcohol was my trigger. In a way, it's why I'm here talking to you, now.'

'In what sense?'

'Before I started coming here for therapy, there was a crisis because I had gone out with a couple of girlfriends and got drunk. Naturally, I ended up going home with a man and having the same unsatisfactory sex as before. I felt bad about it and I told Lee. He was furious. I remember him standing in the kitchen and me trying to hug him. He firmly removed my hands from his body and said, "I'm angry now! Stay away. I don't want to hurt you, so stay away from me. I'm not going to leave. I know you did this because you're self-destructive, but you won't be sleeping with me tonight."'

'How did that make you feel?'

'Because love and sex are the same thing to me, it was unbearable. To be denied his body was devastating. I cried, I pleaded but he told me I would sleep in the spare room and he would sleep in the main bedroom, where he would lock the door. He said it was for my own protection.'

'Punishment?'

'No. I think he was genuinely afraid he would hit me. But I'm very determined. Halfway through the night, I managed to turn the lock with a knife and got into the room where he was sleeping. I took my clothes off and got into bed with him. "I told you to leave me alone," he said but I just turned on my side and ignored him. Then I told him I wasn't staying out there on my own any more because it made me sad. That's when the rough sex episode occurred.'

'And he then told you, you needed to go to therapy?'

'He was right – and that's why I'm here. But he still doesn't know about my father.'

'When did your father's molestation end? How old were you?'

'I was fourteen. I told him if he didn't stop I would cut his throat when he was asleep and by then I was so crazy and out of control he believed I just might do it. By then, he was also afraid that I would get pregnant and the whole story would come out. When I was sixteen, I ran away. When I was eleven, my father organiszed a surprise birthday party for me. He invited every girl in my class. Probably because he was looking for a replacement for me. Although there is no proof. I was increasingly damaged and increasingly rebellious and I suspect he wanted to study potential prey among my schoolmates, even though he liked them younger than eleven. Eleven was already too old for his tastes. From eight to ten, was his ideal range. About twenty girls turned up to our house clutching presents, dressed in what would once have been called their Sunday best. My father was in heaven. His greedy eyes watched my classmates as they played pin the tail on the donkey, musical chairs (songs included gems from Flock of Seagulls, Bronski Beat, Spandau Ballet) and ate plate after plate of junk food. I was in a state of high anxiety. If a girl needed to go to the toilet, I would actually take her to the toilet and lurk around in case my father did anything stupid. I had such low self-esteem by this time that I was amazed anyone had accepted the invitation. It never happened again and I was relieved. I felt responsible for my predatory, irresponsible father in a way he never felt responsible for me. Apart from his obsession with my education and my literary training, he was a disaster as a father and made me an emotional cripple to satisfy his sexual appetites, without a single twinge of conscience. You asked me to write down my dreams last time I was here. I've started recording them in a notebook. I had a nightmare…'

'I thought you were doing better in that area,' said my therapist.

'I was, but it's always one step forward and two steps back.'

'Tell me about it,' she said, uncapping her fountain pen and beginning to write.

'I dreamed about my father. We were in a blood-red room. I was lying on a bed with a silky purple cover on it. I was naked. My father came in and got on the bed with me, started having sex with me. He lay on top of me and I could feel him putting his penis into me. As my father had sex with me, Lee suddenly appeared. He got on the bed too. My father moved aside and Lee started having sex with me. They were smiling at each other as if they were friends or as if it was all a joke. I woke up crying and having a panic attack. Lee tried to calm me down but I was inconsolable. I felt so betrayed. You know how when you have a bad dream and you wake up, for a couple of minutes you think it's true, that it really happened. I was almost hysterical, so Lee gave me a Valium and I was able to go back to sleep after that. But I felt quite depressed the next day.'

'Well, I think this was clearly your subconscious telling you to move on,' said my therapist. 'Your father has been superseded by Lee in your life and in your sex life. Now you just need to make the necessary mental and emotional adjustments.'

But I didn't have her confidence that the situation would be easy to resolve or that it could be resolved. 'But why were they smiling at each other?'

'You can't take these things literally. Things happen in dreams as they happen. Everything in a dream can't be interpreted in some kind of logical universe because in dreams we are untethered from conscience and from morality and from convention. It may be that you're afraid, subconsciously, that Lee will harm your father or even kill him and so in the dream they are friendly and smiling. That would be, in that interpretation, a shield for you. Something your subconscious put there to protect you from a big fear you have, but are not conscious of in your waking life.'

'That makes me feel better,' I told her. 'That was what gave me the panic attack, I think. The idea that they're both men, so they're in it together, or something. It upset me so much. I had a flashback a few days ago, too,' I told her. 'I think it was triggered by the nightmare. I was in the supermarket looking for tampons, actually. Perhaps the tampons were involved,' I managed to laugh, but these things are always very distressing when they happen.

'I was wandering down one of the aisles trying to find the cosmetics and toiletries and all of a sudden I was back in the house with my father and he was bathing me. I was literally back in that bathtub in that bathroom with the blue plastic curtains on the windows with his hands moving the washer slowly over my body and washing between my legs. I started to shake. I was so weak I felt as if I would collapse. I broke out in a sweat. I couldn't see where I was going because I was in the bathtub, literally. All I could see was the blue plastic curtains and the sun shining on them and putting the patterns of the fish on them on my bare skin.'

'How did you cope?' said my therapist with a look of pity and pain on her face.

I often wondered how she did her job, how she survived her job at all.

'I did what you told me to do: stop moving and just slowly breathe in and out, in and out. After a while, it went away but I was a mess. Covered in sweat and shaking. No one noticed. It's the ultimate experience of being alone in a crowd.'

Lee and I went to the pub. A pub near a beach. Sitting out there near the ocean and sipping Chardonnay, I was having a rare moment of peace. I knew he loved me even though it was the most ridiculous thing I could imagine. I regarded myself as some kind of pond life, but much less useful than algae. And yet, I looked at the tiny black mole near his mouth that I had kissed so many times. I couldn't love him properly yet. Someday I hoped I would love him the way he deserved. It seemed a worthwhile goal. He would do anything I wanted. Once, I told him, 'You may very well have the sweetest little arse in the world.' So he lay down beside me naked and turned his back on me so I could caress his gorgeous, smooth flanks. Another time, he didn't want sex because he was too tired – a rare occurrence – but I said, 'Oh, that's all right. I really just want skin and warmth.' So he stripped and lay beside me half asleep while I put my hands and my face all over his naked body. I loved him when he did those things but I didn't think I loved him the way he deserved to be loved. I was still too selfish and dysfunctional to do it.

Then out of nowhere came the news of my father's death. We didn't speak, so if he had been sick I wouldn't have known. I should have been glad but I was distraught and found myself sobbing on and off for days. He had died of a heart attack in his office at the university, surrounded by books. The only things he really loved. It meant I would have to go to his funeral and I didn't know how I could do it. There were all those people to face who had no idea he had molested me.

The therapist fitted me in for an emergency consultation. 'You need to go to the funeral. You need closure,' she told me.

'But does anyone ever really have closure? Do they ever really get it?'

'Staying away will only set your recovery back,' she told me with a steely look and I knew that if I wimped out she would lose respect for me.

I realised for the first time how much I wanted her respect.

'Okay, I'll go.'

It meant a trip to the shops to buy something black and sensible to wear to the funeral. I managed to find a suit that was affordable. I refused to wear a hat as if my father was the prime minister or something.

At the church on the day of the funeral, it looked as if a large group of crows had decided to go to church. Black everywhere, except for on the coffin; the whole funeral had been arranged by his girlfriend. She looked about twenty. Less than a third of his age. The coffin was pale gold wood and it was covered by a large floral arrangement of white lillies.

The funeral itself passed in a blur. I can't remember anything about it. But I do remember standing at the graveside, crying while Lee held my hand and produced a small packet of tissues and tears and snot ran down my face as far as my chin. I cleaned myself up. And then my father was gone, the coffin was lowered down on ropes, I threw dirt on it. The monster was no more.

As we walked back up to the car, I told Lee, 'There's no way I'm going to the morning tea. I just can't.'

He nodded.

We drove out of the graveyard and as we drove along I told him what my father had done to me. At first he looked incredulous, then he cried. But my eyes were dry. I would not let my father rule my life any more. From now on, it would just be Lee in my bed, not Lee and my father. My father would be sleeping with the worms. My therapist had told me that hate was a wasted emotion and she was probably right. But I still hoped there was a hell and that he would go there.

King Crab

When I was twelve, my mother got cancer. It was 1966, the Vietnam War was on TV every night, and no one really seemed to have much idea why the war was happening, so I accepted on that basis that disasters just happened. Not that anyone admitted that my mother's situation was a disaster. It was discussed behind closed doors, but I was protected. It didn't matter. I knew everything and especially the things they didn't want me to know. My mother had a tumour on her thyroid and it was malignant. There was some complication and they couldn't operate. She was going to be in hospital for weeks having radiation and chemotherapy.

Dad and I were living in a borrowed beach house about a half-hour drive from the hospital. It had been loaned by Dad's mate Greg. He was a wheeler-dealer always buying and selling things he had acquired in mysterious ways. So it wasn't that surprising that he turned up one day with a king crab – a huge thing built like a tank. Its claws were bound but it was still alive, so it was moving its claws around – or trying to. It had tiny eyes which I imagined were focused on me, furiously, as if I was to blame for its suffering. It had huge, meaty claws, sprinkled with red decoration and tipped with black. I knew that in the zodiac, the sign of cancer was symbolised by a crab, so the link between him and my mother's disease was there from the minute I set eyes on it.

We had left our farm in the care of Dad's brother, Kevin, and I was determined to get back there, back to the cows and the little white farmhouse that had been my world until Mum got sick. And it was simply unthinkable that we would go back there without Mum. King Crab, as I thought of him, was put into the tub in the laundry and I suppose my father planned to make him into our dinner the next day. I decided that given that a crab had my mother held hostage in the hospital, killing and eating this crab would be very bad juju. I became convinced that it would doom my mother.

The huge crustacean focused his tiny eyes on me and made impatient gestures as I formulated a plan to free him. I could hear the hum of Dad and Greg's conversation. I knew what they would be talking about. It wasn't hard to imagine. How foolish they were, I told myself, to think that killing and eating this crab would not have terrible consequences. I knew I had to act.

After Greg left, Dad seemed listless. Talking about what had happened to Mum only drained him of hope, I could see that.

'I think I'll have a lie down, Alan,' he said with the ghost of a smile and he went into the bedroom and shut the door.

I could hear King Crab rattling around in the tub demanding his freedom. I would give it to him and in exchange he would give me back my mother. I even went into the laundry and looked into what I supposed was his face and said, 'Is that a deal?'

King Crab stopped moving his claws and was completely still. I took this as agreement to my plan. In the beach house, you could hear the ocean. The waves seemed very close and King Crab could hear them too, I supposed. He wanted to go back to his home as much as I did.

As the sun balanced on the ocean like a big orange ball and then sank down into it, extinguished for another day, and darkness fell over the beach house like a net, I waited patiently for Dad to turn in for the night. He wasn't hungry, so we had toasted beetroot sandwiches for tea with ginger beer for me and real beer for him. He watched the news after tea; I couldn't understand why. I thought he had enough troubles of his own without taking on everyone else's. Then he fell asleep on the couch and began to snore.

'Dad', I said, touching his shoulder. 'Go to bed. You're asleep on the couch,' I said, stating the obvious.

'Okay,' he mumbled. 'Turn off the TV, will you? Goodnight.'

He went to bed. I turned off the TV. In the house now, the only sounds were the waves and King Crab rattling and struggling around in the tub, wanting to get back into the ocean. Soon my father's snores chimed in.

I had to transport a very large crab and even though it was pitch-black outside, I had to put him in something. I didn't want random witnesses possibly reporting to my father that they had seen me walking to the beach holding a big crab. I looked out the window up at the sky – the big fat moon was shining like a spoon, to quote a song I wouldn't hear until 1968. I took this as a sign – the moon would light my way. It was after midnight by that time. No one would be around, I hoped.

I found a sturdy shopping bag. I was scared of King Crab. I thought he would struggle and I might drop him-but when I reached out to pick him up and take him out of the tub, he kept perfectly still, the way he had when I asked him about our deal. I slipped him into the bag, found the key to the back door and let myself out, carefully putting the key in the pocket of my jeans. I had grabbed the kitchen scissors on my way out and I put them in another pocket. I would need them to cut his bonds once we reached the beach.

I knew the way to the beach very well. Dad and I took a walk there most days. I saw no one as I trudged along with the crab in the shopping bag. I was impatient to reach the beach and free him because then I knew my mother would get better. The crab had been still but as we got closer to the beach, he began to move around. I held the bag tighter. I mustn't drop him. If I did, his shell might crack. I knew next to nothing about crabs but I knew a cracked shell would not be good. And the deal was that he be delivered alive to the ocean. Otherwise it wouldn't work.

At last the ocean came in sight. The moon shone a silver road across the ocean as the waves rolled and crashed to shore. King Crab was now doing a jig but I had to cut his bonds and I thought as close to the ocean as possible was the best way to do it. So I walked towards the ocean thinking how nice it would be to walk along the silver road that stretched out before me, glowing like silk on the ocean. Down I went on to the beach, the waves roaring in my ears.

I took the scissors out of my pocket and reached into the bag and cut the bonds that bound King Crab's claws. Then I tipped him out on to the beach. He looked at me with his mask of a face. Then he did a sideways charge into the ocean and was swallowed by the waves. I stood there for a minute under the big fat moon that was shining like a spoon. Then I put the scissors in my pocket, picked up the shopping bag and went back up the cold, soft dunes to the road. I walked back through the empty streets certain my mother would live.

We had five good years after that. We went back to the farm. Back to the cows and the little white farm house. Back to normality. My mother was pale and her hair had fallen out but back on the farm colour returned to her face and her hair grew back.

My father had stared in disbelief at the empty tub the morning after my walk to the beach in the dark. 'Where's the crab?' he yelled. 'Did the damn thing escape?'

I tried to look innocent but my father knew. I thought he would be angry but he burst out laughing. It was the first time I had heard him laugh in months.

'You let it go, didn't you? I suppose next you'll be a vegetarian.'

I shook my head.

'Okay, have a shower and we'll go and see Mum.' He was actually smiling.

My mother died, of course she did – five years later. But I've always been sure King Crab thought he kept his part of the bargain. He probably would have said, 'I never promised you forever.' And, of course, no one can. I often thought of the crab over the years, out there in the ocean and wondered if, five years after I released him, he was caught again. At which point our deal was null and void. But that's magical thinking: something only a twelve-year-old boy with a sick mother would believe. That's what I tell myself.

Modern Love

Days of turmoil, days of desperation. It's the norm now. Every day, we live surrounded by shape-shifters and the ground is shifting under our feet as we walk. No certainty. Anywhere. There is a dazzling array of choices – it seems infinite. And yet everything depends, we are told, on finding the person who is 'the one' while everything militates against it. The one can become more than one and, for some people, many more than one. People run the streets like mad dogs scenting pleasure the way a foxhound scents the fox. How is poor love to survive such hedonism and such a universal mania for acquisition? Choices can choke you. The certainties that were taken for granted once are gone. You have to be adaptable but adapting to things you don't want leads to chaos and unhappiness. This is what I learned

The nineteenth-century novelist, George Eliot (Marian Evans) lived in 'sin' in Victorian England and found the relationship between a man and a woman as important as the relationship between the human race and God had once been. Her relationship with George Lewes (her lover) she described as 'profoundly serious'. She had something to rebel against. Now there is nothing to rebel against. You say there's no God? I agree. You say you live in an unmarried *ménage à trois*? Good for you. The rebellion now is to believe in God and have a totally conventional sex life and boring domestic arrangements.

I had cause to ponder a lot of things when I decided to become pregnant at the age of forty. I didn't tell my boyfriend, Ray. I just stopped taking the pill. I was pre-menopausal so there was a small chance that I would get pregnant but I didn't actually think I would. Two months later, I was pregnant. 'Meant to be', I thought. 'But I won't tell Ray until I'm sure.'

This didn't quite work out. When I was three months pregnant, I was hospitalised with a nasty virus that gave me pneumonia. I was put on oxygen and soon I was forced to tell them that I was pregnant. They needed to know so they wouldn't give me some medication that wrecked all my scheming and damaged the baby or gave me a miscarriage.

Inevitably, Ray found out. He was incandescent with rage. Only then did I realise what I had done. Ray felt betrayed, even violated. He acted as if his sperm was his property, even when it was in my body. I didn't know the legal position but I was pretty sure he couldn't sue. Obviously there were still things to rebel against. And stealing sperm (as he saw it) was one of them. Ray was a perfect candidate for fatherhood. He was healthy, he was thirty-seven and he was very good looking. He was in IT and I thought he was intelligent – although his immoderate reaction to the news that we would be parents seemed to prove otherwise. I had always thought he was even-tempered. But I had broken a taboo – his own personal taboo: on me having his child by stealth.

Home from the hospital and feeling profoundly depressed, I had no defence.

'Why'd you do it?' he said.

Putting me in mind of the Marianne Faithfull song of the same name. It deals with infidelity and is laced with profanities. Ray was treating me as if I had betrayed him, so it was applicable.

'I forgot to have a child,' I told him. 'And now I want one.' I was completely unrepentant. I thought he would understand a woman's need to have a child. I was wrong.

'Without asking me? By going behind my back?'

The image of me conceiving behind his back was hilarious but I didn't dare laugh. When he was angry, his eyes went from blue to grey. They were the colour of slate as he spoke. He saw what I had done as an attack on his sovereignty. As if his sperm were a battalion of soldiers and I had carried out a night time raid. The reasons I didn't tell him what I was doing were complex. I suspected he would be completely opposed and would talk me out of it. He was very articulate and forceful in argument.

It was also an expensive business having a child, one he would not want to pay for. I regarded the sperm as my property, once deposited in me – a view he would not accept.

As I thought about it, I decided this was a stupid argument, easily countered by Ray talking about trust. I had thought it was highly unlikely that I would get pregnant at my age by normal means. I did, however. Did my right to bear a child trump Ray's right to know and to consent? I believed it did because I had become one of those desperate women obsessed with having a child by any means. Ray's response to this was to go on a sex strike. I was amazed. Normally he couldn't do without, now suddenly he could. The thought of the unwanted child made him frigid.

This led to a quite amusing (in terms of black humour) visit to a huge shopping centre with a plethora of coffee shops and boutiques.

We were in one of the coffee shops having an ordinary conversation about whether or not we should buy a better coffee machine for the kitchen when he suddenly said to me, 'You should apologise for what you did.'

'Apologise? For wanting to have a baby with a man I love? That's never going to happen.'

'Not for wanting a baby and maybe not for getting pregnant but you should apologise for how you went about it,' he said, giving me a meaningful look and fixing me with his suddenly grey eyes.

'No. I'm not apologising.'

'You have to. If you don't, I can't forgive you and I can never trust you again.'

This was serious stuff. I remembered something I had read in Henry Miller's *Sexus* about human beings and choice: 'We carry heaven and hell within us; we are cosmogonic builders. We have choice – and all creation is our range.' To apologise is also a choice; one I was determined not to make. The choice to get pregnant had been made and I couldn't take it back. I felt that was what he was trying to force me to do: to admit I had been wrong. I didn't believe I had.

'You're asking me to repudiate the baby,' I told him.

'No. It's not about the baby. It's about a breach of trust and without trust there's nothing.'

We drank our coffee, when it arrived, in silence. This was dangerous territory. I could very well end up with a baby and no father.

We left the coffee shop and wandered around the vast shopping centre, with its malls, make up boutiques, health food shops, clothes shops, stationery stores. He persisted in demanding I apologise, sometimes in a raised voice which elicited concerned looks from other shoppers passing by. He had a fetish for wholegrain bread, so we wandered into a health food shop to inspect their wares. But nothing could distract him from his obsession: that I apologise for stealing his sperm.

I ignored him for quite some time but just before we reached the car park I decided he was right (to some extent) and I apologised for not telling him, but I assured him I had no regrets about the baby. It was what I wanted and had wanted for quite a while and I was happy I was pregnant. He seemed more or less satisfied with that.

When we got home, he quickly pulled me into the bedroom and undressed me.

He fastened his mouth on a nipple, taking in the whole thing including the areola. 'I read somewhere you should toughen up your nipples before you have a baby in preparation for breastfeeding,' he said, very seriously, gently chewing away. The sex strike was over.

The pregnancy was long. Very long. There were days when I believed I would never not be pregnant again. But eventually I gave birth via Caesarean to a baby girl with abundant black hair and Ray's blue eyes. I thought she was the most beautiful thing in the world. Ray was overwhelmed, I could see it as soon as he held her. The stark reality that he was now a father pressed in on him the way water closes over a drowning man.

'What are we going to call her?' he said with a panic-stricken smile.

'Patrice Clare,' I said without any hesitation.

'Isn't that a boy's name?'

'No, it's a girl's name too. It's French.'

'Oh, okay.'
I hadn't consulted him on names but he seemed not to mind.

When I thought about the end of the sex strike, it reminded me of a scene in *Sexus* (no one in the book is normal and normal things didn't happen to them, except in the physiological sense). Henry, the protagonist of the book, is talking to his mistress, Mona, and she is telling him how she lost her virginity, even though she had a very tough hymen. The man doing the deflowering had promised her a thousand dollars for the privilege of doing the deflowering. She accepted his offer because she was very poor and came from a poor family which depended on her to help support them. It took this man a week to break her hymen. In the end, she lost the plot and pulled him down on top of her and said, 'Fuck, damn you,' because she just wanted that damn hymen gone. She also bit his lips. This got the required result. But I couldn't imagine ever saying, 'Fuck, damn you' to Ray. Or viciously biting his lips either. Henry also calls his wife Maude 'brazen as a pot' at one point – but I am not brazen as a pot.

The work of toughening up my nipples, done by Ray, did not work. The baby was a voracious feeder. Her little jaws went to work like suction machines and soon enough I had a large crack in one nipple. This meant I could hardly bear to put her to that breast and so I neglected to empty it as I should have. Soon enough, also, I had milk fever. My temperature was 103 degrees, I was hallucinating. Ray called the doctor and he did a house call and wrote a prescription for antibiotics. I lay in bed, delirious, and Ray had to take time off work so he could look after the baby and bring her to feed, which was indescribable agony, at least on one side. The doctor had advised me to get a breast pump and express milk out of the sore breast instead of letting the baby feed from it. Ray went out and got the pump and I did as instructed. After three days, the crack had healed and my temperature was back to normal.

I had almost died. I knew this because during one of my hallucinations I saw an endless line of happy, smiling people walking up a long, winding mountain road leading up into the clouds. I was going with them and I was happy too, until I realised I would be leaving Ray and the baby. At this point my Catholicism, so long dormant, if not dead, reasserted itself and I called out to Jesus for help. Immediately, in my hallucination, a huge metal door like a portcullis reared up out of the ground and clanged shut in front of me and I realised I wouldn't be going after all.

Ray went back to work. He looked pale and harried and was monosyllabic when I spoke to him. While the baby was feeding, I reached for a compact lying on the bedside table and inspected my face in its mirror. I was a wreck. I had lifeless, stringy black hair; my skin was very white and made the dark circles under my eyes the colour of coal. My eyes had the expression I suspected you would see in the eyes of a dying deer. I forced myself to get out of bed once the baby was asleep and apply face cream and then make-up. I brushed my wretched, lifeless hair. It was a vast improvement but I was still too weak to do anything much or even to get out of my nightie. But I knew I had to: I had been wearing it for days.

Fascinating to read in a book I found in a bookcase in the house (*Parallel Lives*), that Jane Carlyle absolutely hated her husband Thomas Carlyle, one of those famous British Victorian intellectuals, because by refusing to have sex with her, he had deprived her of the chance to bear children. Another case in the book was that of Effie Gray and John Ruskin (another famous British Victorian intellectual). Ruskin refused to consummate the marriage and also would have deprived her of the chance to have children if she had stayed with him. He not only refused to have sex with her but told her that her body was disgusting and deformed, even though she was in fact a beautiful young woman. Three years after the wedding, she was examined by doctors and found to be still a virgin, which meant that she could have her marriage to Ruskin annulled. She then married John Millais, the pre-Raphaelite artist who became the president of the Royal Academy, and gave birth to eight children.

Thinking about life and choices, I found a passage in *Sexus* where

Henry Miller has 'Ulric' (but it's actually Miller's own beliefs) say that he envies those who have the courage to become artists and accuses 'Macgregor' (a kind of devil's advocate) of denying what it takes to create beauty, 'which is love. Love of life itself, love of life for its own sake.' I spent my time reading and thinking about what I read because I didn't want to think about the look on Ray's face and the fact that he now barely spoke to me.

Things seemed to be looking up when he arrived home from work with flowers. Roses, no less. Pink roses.

'I thought you might like these,' he said with the smile I hadn't seen for weeks.

'They're lovely,' I said, bemused.

The idea that the roses had anything to do with guilt never crossed my mind. He kissed me and I kissed him back. The ice melted away and for a while things were great. But then the baby began teething. She cried with a will for days at a time. An endless, whiny crying that nothing could stop. We hardly slept and Ray was twitchy, pale and very short-tempered. He looked like a man who had been wronged by life. But I thought he thought I had wronged him.

The thing about Henry Miller, writing in *Sexus*, is that he's always right. So often he starts out meandering around but in the end he's always right. For example, 'No one is more helpless than the heroic individual. And no one can produce more tragedy and confusion than such a type. Flashing his sword above the Gordian knot, he promises speedy deliverance. A delusion which ends in an ocean of blood.' How absolutely true this is. As events in the Middle East prove and have always proven. The fact that Western society is now wedded to the idea of the heroic individual as the ideal citizen is why Western society is in a state of turmoil. More relevant to my immediate situation was something in *Parallel Lives*, but I didn't know it yet.

'A man who is dissatisfied (with a relationship) has many ways of distracting himself from his problem.' Then the author goes on, 'But the most direct way for a man to signal (if only to himself) that his relationship is no longer serving his needs, and the classic way to do something about it, is to fall in love with another woman.'

Unbeknown to me, Ray had come up against that hard fact we never want to face. That we are put on earth to produce the next generation, get old and die. Everything else we achieve is to hide this fact from ourselves and, since men resent it much more than women, a baby's arrival is always in some sense a crisis for them. Suddenly they are not the younger generation-they have been replaced. And, of course, the more we try to forget nature's true purpose for us, to resist it or subvert it, the further we move away from our own humanity and our rightful place in nature. Also, the emptier we become. And we fill that emptiness with 'products' or with 'kicks' – the jolt of sex or drugs.

The affair went on for months before I found out. But, in time, Ray came to understand what Henry Miller already understood in the forties: 'The man who must conquer the woman, subjugate her, bend her to his will – is he not the slave of his slave?' The girl in question was twenty-five. Gravity had not yet laid a hand on her and I spied on her from time to time (watching her emerge to go to lunch during work hours) once I knew about her. She was an ordinary-looking girl. Brown hair, brown eyes and more on the plain side than anything else. But she had a lovely smile that lit up her face. She worked in an insurance office. At first, Ray didn't know I knew. I had found out by reading his emails. Some of them bordered on pornography and they had the name and address of the insurance company on them. Sent in work time. The question was, would he leave me and his child and set up house with this plain, pornographically adept person?

One day I followed her to see if she was meeting him in her lunch hour, but she just went to the park, sat on a bench in the sun and ate some sandwiches. She was thrifty. He would like that. I looked at her mouth and thought, 'He has kissed that mouth, put his tongue in it. Spread those nice tanned legs of hers and plunged into the warm mystery of her vagina. Sucked and bitten those perky little breasts.' One way or another, I was in a bad way. I watched her for half an hour and then she got up and walked off, presumably back to the insurance building. I didn't follow her, because I thought it would be too much of a risk. I didn't want her to see me and realize, by the look of distrait desperation on my face, who I was. I went to a coffee shop and ordered coffee and a huge slice of New York cheesecake. Comfort eating at its most basic.

I didn't think you could say of this insurance clerk what Miller said of his wife's cousin, Julie (he really despised her): 'She was just a piece of ass, with about enough intelligence to realise that after a fuck you had to take a douche and if that doesn't work, a darning needle.' If nothing else, this demonstrates the progress that has been made on contraception and abortion – but the despising of women has not really made all that much progress since the forties. Was Ray's bit on the side difficult, not difficult, intelligent, not intelligent? I had no idea. Going by the emails she had sent Ray, she was a practised sexual fantasist but that was certainly not something Ray would see as a negative.

Henry Miller on fear: 'That is the deepest meaning of the word, "human": that we are a link, a bridge, a promise. It is in us that the life process is being carried to fulfilment. We have a tremendous responsibility and it is the gravity of that which awakens our fear.'

Maybe. Maybe not. But one thing was certain. I was afraid. And quite soon it was all unbearable. I couldn't look at Ray without seeing him kissing her mouth, without seeing him lying between her legs or sucking her breasts. I ordered him to leave, which I could do because I had inherited the house from my mother and it was in my name only.

He went white as a ghost.

'Yes,' I told him. 'I know about your little insurance clerk. I know where she works and what she looks like. I was expecting some sexy type but she's quite plain,' I said, leaning into the word 'plain.'

Now his lips were moving as if he was speaking but he wasn't saying anything. Finally he managed, 'You've been so cold. You're so taken up with the baby and you've been sick…'

'My mother had eight children. My father was never unfaithful to her in thought, word or deed. How do you explain that? I can't even have one baby, without you plunging into a crisis and taking up with some other woman.'

'Your father didn't live in such complicated times,' he mumbled, looking at the floor.

'Oh, that's garbage. You just can't be loyal, that's all. You can't cope with the slightest adversity – because you've never had to.'

That night he slept in the spare room. In the morning, he packed a suitcase and left. He didn't take most of his other belongings from the house, saying he would be back for them. It was the far away and the close up. In an art gallery, if you stand back and look at a painting of a field of red poppies, it looks like a field of red poppies: but if you go right up to the canvas and look at it you can see that they're just little blobs of red paint and they look nothing like red poppies. That's what had happened. I had gone too close to the canvas and had seen, not what I was supposed to see, but what was actually there.

Several months later, he phoned me. He and the insurance clerk had gone their separate ways. He realised that he had made a big mistake and he wanted to talk to me. I hadn't slept properly since he left – so some degree of insomnia was now the norm – and I spent most days crying. My maternity leave was nearly up and I was in a financial crisis. The baby was thriving but still teething. I was prepared to listen to what he had to say. I missed him. I missed him humming when he cleaned his teeth, I missed his laugh, I missed the weight of him on me when by some miracle we actually had sex. I even missed the way he could never find his car keys. I missed the smell of his aftershave and the gum he chewed.

We arranged to meet for a meal at a restaurant in the city at seven p.m. I dressed up, in a silver skirt and a black top, wore the only jewellery he had ever given me, a pearl on a silver chain, dressed the baby and caught a bus. Walking down the street to the restaurant with the baby in my arms, I could smell blossoms on the night air because it was spring. I had no hopes, no expectations, only a burning curiosity. How and why had the insurance clerk left his life?

I found the restaurant, a fairyland of blazing lights in the darkness.

He was sitting at a table near the front window, I saw him before he saw me and I could see he had suffered. He looked as if he had recovered from some kind of illness. Pale and wired, he was studying the menu. It was like seeing someone I was related to. My mother or my father. The shock of recognition and the rush of love at the sight of the familiar face. As if we were linked by blood.

'Oh, hello,' he said, looking up and smiling.

'Hello, yourself,' I said, sliding into a chair across from him.

'I'm sorry. I've been stupid,' he said, looking ashamed.

'I'm sorry you've been stupid, too,' I laughed.

Someone in a passing spacecraft would have seen the two of us through the window of the restaurant, me with the baby held close, talking and laughing and they would have wondered what we were so happy about. Because from the spacecraft they could see the pollution, the forests being burned, the palm oil plantations, the shrinking water supplies, the wars, the innumerable crimes and sins being perpetrated against those who can't defend themselves. Being aliens, they would probably not know about love and its power to make the world seem whole.

As Henry Miller wrote, 'The world is a merry-go-round in flames.' But sitting at that table I was in an Omar Khayyam mood: 'Be happy in this moment; this moment is your life.'

Musical Chairs

I had a friend who said that in the music business it's like a game of musical chairs. In the end, those who got famous just wanted to sit on the chair more than the others. It wasn't really about talent at all; more like *Triumph des Willens*. I was one of those who never got to sit on that chair. But music has been my life regardless. More constant than men, dogs or children. Like that band, Weddings, Parties, Anything – that was my CV, with clubs and pubs thrown in. My life has had a sound track.

'Paper Sun', Traffic – where to begin? What doesn't this song do? So black, so nihilistic, the sitar (is it a sitar?) is so absolutely right. Stevie Winwood's voice sounds like that of a forty-year-old man but he couldn't have been much more than twenty. That bluesy, heartbreaking voice. A poke in the eye for every girl who thought she was having good times with a boy that she just met – I was sixteen and I was sure the world was just like that. I already knew the sun was paper and you might think you're having good times but, chances are, you aren't. And of course he leaves her so forlorn. It had to be that way.

'Paint it Black', Rolling Stones – also a dark, dark vision. A depressive wants to paint the whole world black. Sees a red door and wants to paint it black. There will be no colours any more he wants them to turn black. The beat makes you feel as if someone is slowly and then quickly hammering a nail into your head. Mad instruments whirl around the central pounding theme, doing mad things. This is a song that gallops and makes you want to run out of the house and leave town with the circus. But I was sixteen and my mother wouldn't let me when I actually did try to leave town with the circus. She cried and I couldn't do it. The circus needed a nanny but it wasn't going to be me.

'Getting Better', the Beatles – the singer has to admit it's getting better because it can't get no worse. He used to be an angry young man, he was hiding me head in the sand. All of this spoke volumes to me. I was still at school, still living at home but I had started singing at a local teen hangout and freedom was beckoning. Things did seem to be getting better and this song has John Lennon's wicked wit all over it. It encouraged me to laugh at teenage angst and look forward to the freedom that was so close I could smell it. Still sixteen, but feeling better all the time. Better, better, better. The bouncy, rattly guitar on this song is as uplifting as can be. But halfway through the song, when he's lulled you into a false sense of security, Lennon punches you in the head with a slice of social realism. An autobiographical footnote, I'm sure of that. All about how he I used to be cruel to his woman and beat her and kept her apart from the things that she loved. He was mean but he was changing his scene and doing the best that he can. How we all just took this to be a poppy, happy little song is a bit of mystery but that's certainly what I did. John Lennon could never leave pain out of any song and this is no exception. But at sixteen, I took the 'better' and ignored the pain.

'Light my Fire', the Doors, Jim Morrison – the only thing better than Jim Morrison is Jim Morrison in leather pants. But I digress. The organ that matters in this song is not his. The crazy, hallucinogenic playing of Rick Manzarek is what gives this song its brilliance. Written by Robby Krieger and based on an explicit sexual invitation, it grabs the listener by the short and curlies and won't let go. I didn't have a clue about the sexual delirium it describes, being a sixteen-year-old virgin, but of course I had sexual fantasies. Still sixteen but smart enough to know that the biggest whirlwind blowing the 'doors' around was not Ray Manzarek but the broody, pouting Jim Morrison who sang this song in his high-pitched voice, only going into deep and gravelly mode when he sang, 'Come on baby light my fire'. Millions of teenage girls would have loved to give him what he wanted. Not me. I knew my limits. Even in fantasy.

'Masters of War', Bob Dylan – the Vietnam War. To quote the catchphrase of the time, 'what a drag'. This song is a cry of rage and it's im-

shipped off to Australia, where many of them were enslaved by the Christian Brothers and sexually molested. John Lennon may have gotten some things wrong in his life but this song is not one of them. The words burn like acid and stay with you.

'Rainy Days and Mondays', the Carpenters (1971) – the year this came out was the year the lover and I split up (before getting married in 1972). I was actually talkin' to myself and feelin' old. Frowning came naturally and the words 'moon', 'June' and 'tune' were replaced with 'rainy', 'Monday', 'lonely' and 'clown' and 'down'. Yes. That was exactly what it felt like. As if one layer of skin had been removed and everything hurt.

'Maggie Mae', Rod Stewart – in an interview, Stewart told the true story of what inspired this song. He was at a jazz festival in the early sixties and an 'older' woman, his very first sex partner, pulled him into a tent, 'had her way' with him and then threw him out. The song begins with a mandolin being strummed sweetly, but that soon gives way to an electric guitar and Stewart's rough voice, seemingly a voice that has been marinated in scotch for years, demanding that Maggie wake up because he has something to say to her. He goes on. At length. Tells her that the morning sun when it's in her face shows her age but he doesn't care – to him she's everything. Or so he says. When he tells her all he needed was a friend to lend a guiding hand, the double entendre is all too clear. He chides her for wrecking his bed and in the morning kicking him in the head; but we know his complaint is not serious because after all she was such a demanding lover that she wore him out. And he loved it. In 1971 when this came out, I was living in a flat near a railway line in Brisbane. I had just had a year-long affair and it had ended badly. Each morning, I would turn on the radio while I was still in bed and Rod Stewart's rough, raw and very male voice would demand that Maggie wake up because he thought he had something to say to her. It would remind me of the lost paradise that was the affair. The sexual energy in this song reminded me that I was not living vicariously any more. I was young and I was experiencing great pleasure and great pain. The mandolin at the beginning of 'Maggie Mae' only had to ring out for me to experience in memory every sleepless night spent making love and every day spent sobbing since the affair had ended. Rod never wrote a song as good as this again. Probably because it was based on a true story which involved his first experience of sex. He sums it up when he sings, kidding on that square, that Maggie Mae stole his heart but he loves her anyway. Exactly.

'Your Move', Yes – this also came out in 1971. Another song with an organ crashing away. But what makes this song unforgettable – one of those songs that can transport you in an instant back to where you were in the life when you first heard it – is the voice of the vocalist, Jon Anderson. I believe the organ music was courtesy of Rick Wakeman, who later became somewhat of a music legend. There is also a flute adding pretty, flighty touches to the song as an antidote to Wakeman's possessed organ playing. It's all about someone on the brink of seizing the moment with elements of 'Alice in Wonderland' thrown in – always a winner. The singer urges this person (presumably himself) to make a move on the chessboard of life and to make the White Queen run so fast that she won't be able to make this person a wife – which would only be a distraction and stop him from perfecting his Karma – or whatever. And it tips its hat to an early version of greed is good when it suggests that the ultimate goal is for us to capture as much as we can. Capture what? Could be money, could be sex – either way, the song is cool, clinical and unlike anything else I had ever heard before 1971. At the end of the song, Rick Wakeman moves in like an occupying army with powerful crashing chords. Somehow it all works. As in all the best pop songs, disparate forces come together and it seems as if they were meant to be together. It was indeed my move. My life lay before me. What would I do with it? The player on the other side of the chessboard, the man I had lost and wanted back, had to make his move. That line about make you a wife was most applicable. I can't help wondering if the slogan for the ALP campaign of Gough Whitlam, 'It's time', wasn't inspired by that repeated line of 'it's time, it's time' in 'Your Move'.

'You're so Vain', Carly Simon – this song came out in 1972, the same year I got married, finally, to the man I thought I had lost. Little did I know that it summed up my new husband pretty well. It pumped out of the radio on rotation until I knew the words by heart but I never discovered the full and complete Carly Simon until I bought her *No Secrets* album. Yes, indeed. But I was too much in love to see the similarities. How in love? I thought 'Close to You' (1970, Carpenters) was about him. I listened to the Carpenters sweetly singing about stars falling from the sky and being close to your love object and it all fitted exactly with my experience of being with him.

'Like a Hurricane', Neil Young – this may be the most romantic song ever played by Neil Young as a form of Blitzkrieg. In 1982 in Berlin (of all places) he laid waste to this song on an electric guitar like a man possessed. But the lyrics are as delicate as filigree – almost feminine in their delicacy. The girl he sees in a crowded, smoke-filled bar is, in his imagination, walking from star to star. There's even a pun on the idea of the eye of the storm when he tells her that there's calm in her eyes. And the love seems unrequited at first because he wants to love her but she's like a hurricane and he gets blown away by her power. He's a dreamer but he tells her she's a dream (so they're a perfect match). When she leans towards him to kiss him, he describes that perfect moment when time ceases to exist, that anyone in love experiences sooner or later. Neil Young's voice is so lost, so broken, so innocent that every dream of love anyone ever had crystallises as he sings. In 1982 while he was dancing with a guitar on stage before thousands and thousands of people, I had a new baby and didn't even have the sense to buy disposable nappies, so I was knee-deep in buckets of soaking, shitty nappies. He had the dream, I had an exhausting nightmare of sleepless nights and sore nipples. I even wrote a poem about this song. It's so romantic it seemed to require it. I compared it to heroin – and it's true that I can never just play it once.

'Beautiful Boy', John Lennon – this was a kind of prophetic song. I didn't have a baby in 1980, the year this came out, but when I did in 1981, every word of the song rang true. I wanted to say to my son too that he should close his eyes and have no fear and that any monster that came near him would soon be on the run. I wanted to sing to him that he was a beautiful, beautiful boy. And then he echoes that long-ago song from when he was a Beatle: he tells his baby son to say a little prayer before he goes to sleep and that every day is getting better and better. I even called my son Sean. The most poignant line in this song is when he tells Sean Lennon that he can hardly wait to see him come of age. He never did: a maniac killed him before he got the chance. And how deeply ironic that he tells his son that life is what happens to you while you're busy making other plans because that is exactly what happened to John Lennon. Making an album, back with Yoko, so full of love for his son and then bang, bang you're dead. They are now attributing those lines to *Reader's Digest* but I don't believe it. John Lennon probably never read *Reader's Digest* in his life and it's so typically Lennon, so much his view of the world, and so much what happened to him in his own life, that I believe it came from him – the same as all the rest of this remarkable and beautiful song.

'Pride', U2 – so relevant to the 'troubles' in Ireland which led to IRA attacks in Britain. This song is a plea for love in the face of vicious, sectarian hatred. When Bono screams out, 'In the name of love', you feel it in your bones. And when he croons in the middle of the song, it sounds like a dystopian lullaby sung for the children of Ireland, who feature so heavily in the video they made for the song. I was very aware of what was happening in Ireland. My mother's family hailed from County Cork. The image of a leader full of love who ends up crucified on a barbed-wire fence could refer to almost any Irish leader of the past – or Jesus. There has always been more than enough betrayal to go around in Irish history and the images of a man crucified on a barbed-wire fence and being betrayed with a kiss are perfect – so very Catholic. Thatcher was in power when this song came out in 1984. A plea for Christianity to prevail in an obsessively Christian country which has lost its Christian values to a blood thirsty and destructive political and religious elite and the British establishment. Finally, in 1998, the Irish people at last got to vote in a referendum and demanded peace. And got it. The devil may have all the best tunes, but not in this song.

'Smells like Teen Spirit', 'Come as you Are', 'Lithium', Nirvana – the band that typified the nineties for me was Nirvana. 'Smells like Teen Spirit', 'Come as you Are', 'Lithium' pumped out constantly from radios during the nineties. Kurt Cobain's voice is a high, clear challenge, like John Lennon singing 'Jealous Guy', except for when he goes into a growl that's a cross between a yell and a sigh He was also what used to be called 'easy on the eye' with his blue eyes, blond hair and movie-star face. In 'Come as you Are', he sings over and over that he hasn't got a gun but in the end he did have a gun and he used it to kill himself. In 'Lithium', he sings that he's not gonna crack but in the end he did crack. Proving yet again that money and fame don't bind your wounds. Amazingly in this song he also sings that he's not only ugly but so ugly. Sadly he probably did believe he was ugly. Like the society around him, he was so damaged he couldn't be saved and there was only one way they could both go – down.

'Into Temptation', 'Fall at your Feet', 'It's only Natural', Crowded House – but it was Crowded House that had my heart. Neil Finn: his fantastic voice, his genius for melody and the songs he created seemingly without end. His songs are tough but also romantic – just like his native New Zealand. In 1991, I watched in horror as the US invaded Iraq – and not for the last time either. In 1992, the Bosnian War unfolded. Just when war seemed to be redundant, it made a comeback. The romantic, quirky, fantastical songs of Crowded House were an antidote. You could listen to Neil singing about being lured into temptation or falling at some woman's feet or how he wants to be read like a book that's fallen down between some woman's knees. The news was an endless horror story but Neil Finn's music swept you away to beauty and romance and you could forget that in Bosnia and Iraq innocent civilians were being slaughtered. At least for as long as you were listening to Crowded House.

'Jeremy', Pearl Jam – as an anthem for the nineties, it's hard to go past this song. The nineties embodied Oscar Wilde's description of people who 'know the cost of everything and the value of nothing'. That was the nineties – economically and socially. These lyrics are the nineties too.

There is the seemingly innocent child's drawing of Jeremy standing on top of a mountain, with a lemon yellow sun and his arms raised in a V. But down below in the valley, dead bodies lie in pools of blood. His father wasn't paying attention and his mother didn't care and so it was that the evil-doers were all powerful in Jeremy's world – or so it must have seemed to him. When Jeremy speaks in class, it is to reply to the relentless bullying from which he was never protected. Jeremy is the story of Jeremy Delle, who was bullied daily by the classmates at his Texas school. No one did anything to help him or protect him. So he shot himself in front of the entire class. He 'spoke' in class but, like a true Texan, he let his gun do the talking. The boy who seemed to his classmates to be a harmless and vulnerable loser, ripe for bullying, made his last defiant gesture. *Lord of the Flies* became an operating manual in the nineties; the savages were infiltrating politics. The right may have begun their war on the Clintons in the nineties but it has continued to the present day and they have even managed to drag the Russians into it.

And that's where music ended for me. Since the noughties, music has degenerated into more or less triviality and incoherence. The new music is not part of my life. My soundtrack is still the music of the sixties, seventies, eighties and nineties. I listen to it daily and I live my life by its lyrics. They are my history and my future, told in song by people I will never meet but who seem to know me.

Pretenders

Why did I do it? I'd just had a baby which I was still breastfeeding. I had a husband, another child and a house to run but, nothing daunted, the lure of the footlights was too much for me. Shakespeare paid homage to the amateur actor in *A Midsummer Night's Dream* and such a one was I.

'We can't get anyone to play Marmee in *Little Women*,' my friend Greta told me. She and her husband Henry ran the local repertory theatre. 'Will you do it?'

I could tell by her face that she had her heart set on me doing the role. 'I suppose…'

'Great! Here's the script.'

I was such a fool I didn't even read the script. The part had been handed to me, so I didn't bother, I simply waited until the first read-through in a freezing room under the theatre, at which point I discovered that Marmee was in every scene bar one (when she went to Washington) and there were reams of lines to learn. We couldn't rehearse in the theatre because another play was being rehearsed there – *Inspector Hound* – so we were stuck in this room like a refrigerator. Learning all those lines was the least of my problems. I not only had to know the lines, I had to be able to speak them as Marmee, in character in other words. This proved to be a challenge because after all I had no training and no experience but then neither did the ten-strong cast. Some of them actually had acting ability, though, which was fortunate for them because the director, a ferocious woman who was about six foot two, treated us as if we were professional actors. Near enough was not good enough. I was treated with contempt by all of them. Greta had handed me the role because I was her friend and I looked good. I wasn't old enough for the role and my acting ability was minimal. Calling it minimal was actually kind.

But my woes were nothing by comparison with a poor unfortunate chubby girl (a high school student, like all of them) who was bullied and persecuted at every opportunity by everyone except me. She was playing Beth, who died in the play, and it was indeed a merciful release. I bit my tongue and didn't defend poor Beth. I was in a bad situation myself and decided discretion was the better part of valour. This girl had buck teeth of a mossy green colour and had no idea how to defend herself from her 'Lord of the Flies' persecutors. The fact that she could actually act did her no good at all. Huddled in the Arctic downstairs room, rugged up in three layers of clothes, a scarf, gloves and tights and boots and struggling through the script was a nightmare. But strangely it never occurred to me to throw in the towel: once I had committed to a certain course of action, I stuck to it doggedly.

The director was a relatively benign presence to begin with. No doubt she thought I would improve. The thought never occurred to her that that I couldn't and wouldn't. So, enthusiastically, we went through scene after scene over and over again. The director was patient. Patiently she explained things to me. Marmee's age, social status, her place at the centre of the play, the warmth and motherliness she must display. I heard every word she said but all too often I was reminded of the saying that when you talk to a dog all it hears is its name. She could never make me translate my understanding of what she said into my performance. It was all the stranger because I had just had a baby boy who I loved tenderly but the ability to incorporate that into the role was missing in action. I nodded energetically as she spoke and she must have believed that telling me these things would eventually result in a workmanlike performance – brilliant or even good were not going to happen. Greta had stuck her with a dud and she just had to make the best of it. It was like watching everything being put in place for a slow-motion train wreck and feeling as if you were driving the train.

The boy playing Laurie was perfectly cast and captured the character he was playing perfectly and, seemingly, effortlessly. I hated him for it and also because he usually seemed to be the ringleader in the persecution of Beth. Being young, good-looking and talented was no excuse in my mind for being a shit.

The rehearsals were like being locked in Hitler's bunker with good-looking young psychopaths. The guy cast as my husband (Mr March) despised me and once shoved me to one side when he was supposed to offer me a tender embrace. How the young psychos laughed at this. They were supposed to be my children: I was supposed to love them but I absolutely hated most of them. The girls playing Jo and Amy were pretty and competent and didn't go out of their way to persecute me. I was grateful but I didn't like them – they were too good at acting for that to happen. The only real actress in the entire cast was the middle-aged woman playing Aunt March. She had a voice someone had trained the hell out of and played her role with majestic ease (her grey curls bobbing for emphasis when required). In spite of that, I liked her and she was kind to me. Very kind, as it turned out during the matinee once the play was actually running. More of which later. The gigantic director loved this woman and practically bowed when she passed and never shouted at her or gave her withering looks. Why would she? So we continued, bogged down in minutiae and the fierce winter; struggling with the era (the American civil war) and the costumes we would eventually wear.

'You can't walk like that,' the giant director barked at me one day. 'You'll be wearing a crinoline!'

I couldn't act and now it seemed I couldn't even walk, something I thought I had mastered at twelve months. I backed away from her, muttering, 'Yes, of course,' while picturing her staked out naked on an ant bed.

Soon we were actually in the theatre and on the stage, speaking our lines and making our exits and entrances as we would once the play was running. This was a thrill, but not as big a thrill as it should have been because I soon went down with a fierce throat infection that made me weak, nauseous and bedridden. I was sure it had been brought on by stress and the time spent in the freezing rehearsal room. Adding to the stress was the fact that the director had informed us we would be taking part in a drama festival in another town and performing a scene from the play. I was semi-conscious, lost in feverish anxiety dreams where I fell off the stage and swallowing antibiotics when they went to the drama festival and won every prize, with the strapping director playing Marmee.

I was too sick to care about any of that. My husband brought the baby to feed every four hours and I was hardly even aware it was happening. The only good result of my illness was that the contempt most of my fellow actors felt for me withered away when they realised that the play would be cancelled if I didn't come back. Dress rehearsal was now one week away and opening night only two.

Dress rehearsal was a complete disaster. Everything that could go wrong did. I had returned by then, on trembling legs that could hardly hold me up, still on antibiotics and feeling as if I was on drugs – the illegal kind. But my fellow actors were glad to see me back and greeted me with happy cries that I knew were genuine. Because no one wanted to see the play cancelled. But after the dress rehearsal it seemed almost certain that it would be cancelled anyway. Greta, Henry and the director from hell sat in the front row looking like the three wise monkeys, only much sadder. No one spoke. Down in the dressing room the rumours flew. The play was such a shambles the three wise ones didn't see how it could be put on.

'They think it's better to abandon ship than go down with the *Titanic*,' Aunt March told me in her mellifluous voice with its immaculate vowels. She alone – naturally – had played her role to perfection during the dress rehearsal while the rest of us blundered around like fools, breaking the two cardinal rules of acting: remember your lines and don't bump into the furniture. Fail, on both counts. But for some reason Greta and Henry decided that all our work could not be in vain, especially since I had climbed out of my death bed to come back and play Marmee. They decreed that the show must go on. There is a superstition in the theatre, so I learned much later, that a terrible dress rehearsal means opening night will be wonderful. And so it was, even though one of the girls in a minor role had taken Valium and said her one line with the drone-like quality of a robot. Other than that, it all went perfectly. We knew our lines and I was less wooden than usual and even felt at times that I was in character. The audience clapped like mad and we took three bows.

But unfortunately whoever wrote the play based on the book was clearly not an actor and knew nothing about the reality of staging a play. Unlike Shakespeare, for example. During each performance there came the moment when Marmee had to go to Washington and come back ten years later and walk down a flight of stairs back on to the stage. The problem was that in the time I had allotted to exit, and then make my entrance in entirely different clothes, I had to run down a dark flight of stairs, race through a rabbit warren of hallways until I reached the dressing room and change from head to foot. I never did it without being in a panic that I would miss my entrance and my cue.

And this was when Aunt March came to my rescue during the matinee. There we were, she in her costume and me struggling out of mine and trying to put another one on. She came to help me but it was like one of those horrible dreams where you are running as fast as you can but not moving. Every movement seemed agonisingly slow and I remember watching her desperate face as she pulled my blouse over my head and down, while everything seemed to be in slow motion. Adding to my panic was the fact that I was wearing a wraparound skirt that was only tucked into my pantyhose and not fastened because there was never time. Every time I walked down those stairs, I was sure the skirt would drift down around my ankles, make me trip and send me headlong down the stairs to lie exposed and humiliated in front of the audience.

The play only went for two weeks but it was two weeks of high anxiety, with only one person who cared enough to help me change costume because I had finally snapped when the young psychos were persecuting Beth and told them off. Aunt March had muttered 'Fine young cannibals' under her breath and given me a smile. But the damage was done. My name was mud from then on in the cannibals' camp.

I had put a bottle of champagne in the refrigerator in the theatre kitchen to celebrate the success of the play – and it was a success, garnering a gushingly positive review in the local paper – but by the time it was all over I was so disgusted with the whole thing that I sneaked to the fridge and took the champagne out. I took it home and used it to toast the fact that I had survived the experience of treading the boards. The young psychos watched me silently, contemptuously as I slunk away with the bottle. To hell with them. They weren't drinking my champagne. I drove home with the bottle on the back seat of the car. The dark streets were familiar but deserted. I felt like a piece of space junk moving through space. Cold and alone. I had not hoped for success, only survival, but the play had succeeded. It was me who had failed. Failed to connect with my fellow thespians, failed to keep my mouth shut re Beth, failed to please the director. The sweet, sparkly tone of *A Midsummer Night's Dream* seemed far, far away but I thought you probably had to see acting the way Shakespeare presents it in that play to endure the fact that you needed the hide of a rhinoceros and the constitution of an ox to make a career of it.

Once home, I sipped my lonely glasses of champagne. Husband and children slept on. It took years for me to understand that I had not failed. I had played my part. In acting, as in life, it was enduring that mattered. Knowing that you could fall, that you could fail and going on anyway, is the victory.

Straight

'It's not just the penis,' I told him irritably. 'It's the whole experience of being with a man.'

'Meaning what?' he said, sceptically.

'Their sweet, useless little nipples, their cute little arses, their beautiful legs, body hair, biceps, pecs, muscles overall, their beautiful hands, their voices, the way they smell, the way you smell when they've finished with you. I even like the feeling of semen running down my legs. I wouldn't get this with a woman so I'm not interested. I'm hopelessly straight but I can change if you want me to,' I added as a parting shot.

Paul looked absolutely scandalised. I laughed at him and turned on the coffee machine. His jealousy wasn't cute or funny, it was just tiresome. Was any woman I was friends with now going to be seen as a threat? In spite of me explaining to him why I preferred having sex with men rather than women and swearing that I was straight?

He grew ever more infuriating. When I was in the kitchen, I would hear him coming up the stairs from the rumpus room where he read the newspaper and watched cable. The stairs creaked so I always knew when he was coming. Sometimes hope revived briefly and I would expect him to do something interesting but when he got to the kitchen, did he tell me a funny story, praise my beauty or stick his finger up my pussy and make me purr? No. None of the above. He would just look at me with his stupid suspicious face, as if he expected me to be writhing on the kitchen floor with some woman. I was often rendered speechless by the sight of his paranoid face and he was not prepared to say anything much, for fear of copping another blast of logic from me. So we would stare at each other silently: he with suspicion and me with contempt. A horrible way to live but on our own neither of us could afford the rent we were paying for the townhouse we shared.

It had all started to go bad at his fortieth birthday party, when he found me in the kitchen in the arms of the blonde and beauteous Katie who was (I had no idea) a lesbian. For some reason, she decided I was too, and launched herself at me. I was too shocked to stop her and stood there like a dolt being energetically kissed.

Paul dropped the glass bowl he was carrying to the kitchen on the tiles, where it smashed into a million scintillating shards of crystal. 'What the hell are you doing?' he asked, very softly. He was white as a ghost.

Katie stopped kissing me, blushing fiercely, and left the kitchen. This left me to try to explain things to Paul, whose face had gone from white to red with anger. Downhill all the way from there, except in bed. The belief that I was a lesbian stimulated him to new heights, while producing fierce resentment and disgust at the same time. It was both exhilarating and confusing for me and the stress was wearing me down. I even began to doubt my sexuality, something I had never experienced in my life before. I began to think that I was in fact a lesbian. Paul was convinced that I was and it seemed Katie was too. The thought came to me (I dismissed it at first) that the only way I could know for sure was to go to bed with Katie. How else could I know the truth?

When Paul had finally gone to sleep after treating me to angry sex, no doubt while visualising me in bed with Katie, I would rant to myself that he wanted to have his cake and eat it too. He wanted to punish me for being (as he thought) a lesbian but he also wanted to use the idea of it to become sexually aroused and to increase his own sexual pleasure. On the outside, I was calm but inside I boiled with rage. I felt as if he was treating me like a sex toy and longed to ask him to move out but I couldn't pay the rent on my own and I was in a 'better the devil you know than the devil you don't' frame of mind. I could recall in grim detail every horrible flatmate I had ever had and he was far from being the worst of them.

To make matters worse, Katie had begun stalking me – texting, phoning, messaging me on Facebook. I ignored her lovestruck messages which were trying so hard not to be lovestruck. She was now in a state I recognised all too well. I had often been in that state myself. I had even been in that state about Paul in the beginning. I would go weak in the knees remembering the smell of his aftershave. My pussy ached whenever I thought of his hairy chest and his gorgeous tanned hands. Thinking about his taut little arse almost brought on the vapours. I knew exactly what Katie was going through and I pitied her. It's a delusional state produced by a chemical called PEA, which dissipates, or begins to, around the two-year mark in a relationship. Paul and I had been together almost two years exactly. It was an explanation, but there was more to it than that.

By mistake, I answered a call from Katie – pressed the wrong button, dithering around. When my mobile rings, I panic and flounder around like a fool. I can never remember what I'm supposed to touch to answer calls and consequently answer calls I don't want to take and miss calls I do want to take. And just when I get used to it, my phone becomes out of date and I have to get a new one and start all over again.

Katie's voice was high and nervous. 'Aileen, I need to see you. I need to see you as soon as possible. We have to talk.'

I was feeling annoyed with Paul and took it out on her. 'I'm pretty sure talking's not what you have in mind,' I said, with a carefree laugh.

There was painful silence from her end. 'No, really,' she said at last, 'I have to talk to you.'

'Just as long as you remember it's hard to talk with someone's tongue down your throat.' I actually giggled, then realised that she would interpret it as flirtation.

There was a confused sound from her and then the sound of paper rustling. 'I'm at work,' she said. 'I'll have to go. I need to see you but I'll understand if you don't want to.' She hung up.

I only then noticed that Paul was watching me with the suspicious look that had become his normal way of looking at me. 'Who was that?' he murmured, pretending to be reading the paper.

'It was Katie,' I said.

He stopped pretending to read the paper and stared at me. He stared at me for some time but I gave him no further information and left for work. Let him stew. I had no idea what I was going to do. Meeting Katie would facilitate my plan to go to bed with her to find out if I was gay or not but that was a drastic step and did I even want to know? Not knowing had served me well so far, why rock the boat? In a way, Paul was encouraging me to find out because his hostile, suspicious face was driving me mad and I longed to tell him something that would be a victory for me. Either that I was gay (victory for me in that I had been to bed with a woman and proved I was gay and didn't need Paul) or I wasn't gay (victory for me in that Paul was wrong and had been behaving like a fool). Once victory becomes more important than common sense, you have definitely lost your way.

Katie soon phoned again and this time I agreed to meet her. After I got off the phone, I felt sick when I thought of the implications, but I needed a circuit breaker: something had to change. Leaving would have been the simplest option but it would also have been cowardly. I told myself it was time for me to stop being cowardly. When I sat down at the kitchen table, I noticed my hands were trembling but I was resolved to prove to Paul that I was, or was not, gay. Increasingly, I didn't care what the outcome was, only that there was an outcome. Action versus stasis. If I had to go on living with his crazy suspicions, I thought I would start speaking in tongues. A Freudian slip, of course, to be thinking that.

When I met her in a coffee shop, Katie was obviously excited but very smooth. 'Oh,' she said, 'I hope I didn't cause any trouble.'

I wanted things to stay pleasant so I told her things were fine. A complete lie. Things had never been worse between Paul and me and it was because of her mad kiss. I didn't tell her I myself now wanted to know if I was gay or not or that I considered her the ideal candidate to help me find out. She looked lovely. Her porcelain skin was slightly flushed and her blonde hair washed and shining. She was wearing a black dress with a white band at the neck and the hem. She could have stepped off the cover of a magazine and her poppy red lipstick meant that her mouth was the focal point of my gaze. I found myself staring at her breasts, the tops of which rose slightly above the white band at the neck of her dress; two round, milky

I had only gone to this party because the hostess had phoned me repeatedly and begged me to be there.

'Too many men and not enough women,' she told me, while a blender frantically blended in the background. 'I'm making guacamole dip,' she said over the grinding, crunching shriek of the blender.

I made a last minute decision to go, washed my hair, wore a glittery top and slinky black skirt and treated my lips to fuchsia lipstick I had bought the day before. Diamond studs in my ears, a black choker around my neck and strappy black shoes on my feet and I was out the door. Paul didn't even bother responding when I shouted down the stairs. 'I'm going to a party at Stella's.' Silence. I roared off in the car in a bit of a rage. But now I was sitting in a pergola with a lovely man, sipping white wine and in no kind of rage at all.

By midnight, I was in his bed and any idea that I was gay was put to scorn. If not to the sword. I behaved disgracefully and so did he. I pictured Paul at home, downstairs, asleep in the big red armchair he favoured for reading the newspaper while a movie ran unwatched and had to stop myself laughing. Paul was a man who could drive a woman to other women in desperation, I was sure of that, but that didn't mean I was a lesbian. Or even that I had some kind of sexuality crisis. In all likelihood, he did. Craig was the anti-Paul: he was gentle, skilled and worked hard to please me – and he did.

Lying there the next morning, a study in tanned skin and tangled white sheets, he was everything I thought I wanted. But now I was so cynical I thought he was too good to be true. I thought he had to have some flaw. A wife. A girlfriend. Narcissistic personality disorder. Alcoholism. The list I went through in my mind seemed endless. My clothes, my jewellery, my handbag and my shoes lay in a heap on the floor. Discarded in a frenzy in my eagerness to get into bed and it all seemed like the beginning of something. But what? And would it be good or bad?

'I'll make breakfast,' Craig said, confirming that he was too good to be true.

I decided I would do nothing. I wouldn't phone or text Paul, I would just let things unfold.

When I went home three days later, Paul was frosty but seemed unfazed.

'You stayed at Stella's,' he said. It wasn't a question. He simply assumed that I was 'safe', that no other man would want me, since he didn't.

'No, actually. I met someone at the party and went home with him. I slept with him and I've been with him for three days at his place and now he's asked me to move in with him.'

Paul's face went a dirty grey colour. "You aren't serious?' he said, after a while.

'Yes, I am. That's what happened. So I'll be moving out, which means you'll need to find another flatmate if you want to keep renting this place.'

Only silence from him.

'And I know for sure now that I'm not gay,' I added as he turned to walk away.

He didn't stop and he didn't turn round. I watched him walk away and was sad: for him, for us, for what might have been.

My mobile rang. It was Katie and for once I was able to answer it without any fuss.

'We still on for next week?' she said with girlish excitement.

'No, Katie. I'm sorry. I've met someone else and I'm moving out of the townhouse. His name's Craig. I met him at a party at Stella's. Everything's kind of up in the air.'

There was silence and then a strange noise. It took me a while to realise she was crying. I cast around desperately. What could I say? Nothing I said would comfort her. I realised for the first time how much she had invested in me and the hope of a relationship. PEA was the same in same-sex relationships, so she was in its grip as I had been before, was now and would be again. It was another cruel trick of Mother Nature – she had so many to play on us and most people didn't even know she was fooling them. It was no comfort to know I knew about her tricks. It didn't save me from suffering any more than it would save Katie.

'Katie, I'm not a lesbian. We could never have been together,' I told her, kindly.

She stopped crying and shouted, 'Screw you, you deceitful bitch,' down the phone. Then she hung up.

I smiled. She would be all right. Then I got down my rather battered brown suitcase that had been all over the world with me and began packing. I felt foolishly, uselessly guilty over Katie and Paul. Tomorrow would be different. Better? Worse? Who could say? But it would be different, that much was certain.

Stump

When Stump got elected, there was a collective intake of breath – as if the news of someone's death had been announced. At first, everyone thought it was a joke and they went on thinking that for quite some time. But soon he showed that if he was a joke, it was a joke based on the blackest of black humour. Eisenhower, that two-faced ninny, had at least retained a grip on reality. When Allen Dulles, director of the CIA, wanted to invade Vietnam to help the French out in Dien Bien Phu, Eisenhower said, 'If we do so, the Vietnamese could be expected to transfer their hated of the French to us.' Even Churchill, that inveterate old warmonger, turned Dulles down. 'We have to face the fact that the fortress is lost,' he rumbled. Dulles refused to accept it. Ho was a Communist, so he had to go. It was inconceivable to Dulles that Ho could have the last laugh. A sparrow could not defeat an eagle. Churchill knew that, given the right circumstances, it could. That's what kept him going through the Blitz.

Stump lacked Dulles's craftiness and guile and he lacked Churchill's sophistication and sangfroid. He was simply a delusional fool and revealed it every time he opened his mouth, He constantly made announcements and issued directives. He thought governing a nation and being a CEO were the same thing. People mocked him relentlessly, drew cartoons and photoshopped his head on to the bodies of obese babies, but he just kept going. His German peasant ancestors had known how to keep going – and being wrong never entered his head. Journalists laughed at him and the voters kept saying, 'Who voted for him?' in huge amusement, as if it was all nothing to do with them. But then he started dropping bombs on countries that were already destroyed by wars his predecessors had started – and lost. He boasted about the tonnage of the bombs he dropped as if he was talking about the size of his penis. He was a disaster on every front and no one knew what to do about it. His wife and his sons and daughters quickly became liabilities. His wife to such an extent that she at first refused to move into the White House. They were like people in a minefield – wherever they stepped, there was a media explosion. The disbelief and then the laughter of the public faded away after Stump dropped the bombs. This was serious. A fool was in the White House and that was nothing new, but this fool was more ignorant and more dangerous than any before him. Everyone knew it and hoped for something to remove him. The religious ones prayed for divine intervention.

Stump's knowledge of and understanding of history was extremely limited but it was possible to guess the kinds of things he would approve of. For example, the way Allen Dulles took over control of the making of the animated film version of *Animal Farm*. He changed the ending of Orwell's work so that the animals didn't realise that both sruling groups were corrupt; instead, in Dulles' version, only the pigs are corrupt and patriotic rebels overthrow them. Stump would not have liked that message, necessarily, but taking total control of a masterwork of antitotalitarianism and turning it into something that fits your own totalitarian world view has something so twisted in it, he would have approved had he known of it. Power over others and the exercise of that power was all Stump understood. Absolutism was his norm. Another thing Stump would have loved was that in 1955 Allen Dulles was celebrating the phone tapping tunnel he had had dug in Berlin. Even the fact that it ended in disaster when Soviet agents charged into the tunnel and CIA officers fled in all directions wouldn't have mattered to him. A Soviet mole, the British agent, George Blake, kept the KGB informed and they had monitored it from the start. But Stump would have loved the recklessness and audacity of it.

Stump was ostracised for refusing to shake a European leader's hand and had no way of knowing that Allen Dulles had done the same thing. He turned his back on the Chinese leader Zhou Enlai, almost certainly to avoid shaking a Communist's hand, deeply wounding Zhou, who told the story for years.

Most of the things Stump thought were so shiny and new and all about him, really weren't because most of them had happened before to other leaders in other eras. His historical illiteracy protected him from knowing this. Allen Dulles's vision for America was both corporate and ideological but for Stump everything was corporate. His outlook was terrifyingly simple: America was the best in every way, so America had to rule the roost and the only way America could do that was to rule the globe. Stump's attitude to Russia would have given Allen Dulles the vapours. Stump vaguely understood that America had to have a global enemy to justify its global hegemony but that was already covered – the 'caliphate' was their enemy du jour – so why did they need to be enemies with Russia? Stump the businessman knew how much money there was to be made in Russia and he thought it was pure madness not to get in for a piece of the pie. The CIA was enraged by Stump's buddy-buddy attitude to Russia but he didn't care. He was too foolish to care. The countries of the faux caliphate were poor, so he despised them, except for the ones like Saudi Arabia which were obscenely wealthy.

This was his ideology – money good, no money bad. And in so many ways, it was America's ideology too. The CIA's worldview was not deep or subtle but they played the long game. The faux caliphate would do the trick for now, but why throw away a perfectly good enemy like Russia, which was nuclear-armed and had a formidable army and could always be used to stir up fear? The culture of the CIA was in many ways Dulles's, because for so long he was the CIA. Their normal outlook, like his, was drenched in paranoia and religious righteousness, coupled with a complete distrust of anything or anyone who was not American. They were globalists but they were xenophobic too. White was best and America was God's messenger and God's foot soldier.

Stump was a globalist too, in so far as he would do business anywhere he could make money, but he didn't share the CIA's belief that it knew best. He thought he knew best and that was that. He was a loudmouth and a bully and he was too old to change and too inflexible to learn from those who knew better. The rest of the world watched him with fascinated horror, and prided themselves on the fact that they could never be fooled into electing such a horror. Had Stump had any grasp of history, he would have known that when it came to Vietnam both France and Britain turned away.

The US took the first step towards its destiny throughout the late twentieth and early twenty-first centuries: to do what its allies were too ashamed to do without the fig leaf of cover of the War on Terror, namely to blow up third world countries for profit. Or to simply give them regime change. Allen Dulles had six monsters that he had to destroy: Abenz of Guatemala, Mossadegh of Iran, Castro of Cuba, Patrice Lumumba of the Congo, Ho Chi Minh of Vietnam and finally his own president, John F. Kennedy, who refused to invade Cuba. But these were monsters Dulles chose himself out of his Protestant, far right, Calvinist manias. Stump had his monsters provided for him. Iraq, Afghanistan, Iran, Syria, Libya, Yemen. As Orwell wrote, 'The war was not meant to be won, it was meant to be perpetual.' When Dulles went to war, he meant to win, his God demanded it. Stump had no such goal – he was the perfect president for the Pentagon, if not the CIA, because he was punitive by nature and liked harming other countries simply because he could. The end goal was not the defeat of evil but a healthy balance sheet for the arms corporations – the exercise of power for its own sake. As a corporate animal, that was fine by him.

Stump knew next to nothing about how America ended up bogged down in a war in Vietnam that the Rand Corporation and the Pentagon and the CIA knew from quite early on was unwinnable. The fact that America manoeuvred a leader into place in Vietnam who was a Catholic in a country that was ninety per cent Buddhist was unknown to him. Diem, the chosen leader, had spent the previous two years of his life living in seminaries, one of them in New Jersey and run by Cardinal Spellman. Exiled emperor, Bao Dai, summed Diem up as 'A psychopath who wishes to martyrise himself even at the price of thousands of lives.' All he got wrong was the number – five million Vietnamese died during the Vietnam War.

All of this was a closed book to Stump but he would have said if he was honest, which he almost never was, 'What do all those dusty old history books have to do with me?' History would have been wasted on him, in any case, just as it was wasted on both Allen Dulles, director of the CIA and (John) Foster Dulles, his sibling and secretary of state. Like Stump, they only saw what they wanted to see. Foster Dulles's pronouncement on China now seems to fit much better as a description of America in the twenty-first century: 'Unfortunately there are governments or rulers that do not respect the elemental decencies of international conduct so that they can properly be brought into the organised family of nations.'

At times, the ignorance of Foster Dulles could even give Stump a run for his money. In an interview for the *New York Times* with Walter Lippman, Dulles said this: 'The only Asians who can really fight are the Pakistanis. That's why we need them in the alliance. We could never get along without the Gurkhas.' Lippman told him the Gurkhas weren't Pakistanis. 'Well they may not be Pakistanis, but they're Muslims.' Lippman said they weren't Muslims, they were Hindus. 'No matter!' Foster Dulles said and began talking about the dangers of Communism in Asia. Hardly surprising that he later wanted to use nuclear weapons on China, claiming that they could utterly destroy military targets, without endangering 'civilian centres'. Stump was also profoundly in love with nuclear weapons and also itched to use them on China.

Churchill summed up Dulles with typical wit. 'Foster Dulles is the only case I know of a bull who carries his own China shop around with him.' This was also an accurate description of Stump. Foster Dulles gave an interview to *Life* magazine in 1955 in which he said that his diplomacy was aimed at bringing America to the 'verge of war'.

Stump had no diplomacy but he had the exact same aim from day one of his presidency. Stump also shared the contempt for democracy that was the hallmark of everything the Dulles brothers did. The fact that they knew that Ho Chi Minh would get around eighty per cent of the vote if the election mandated by the Geneva Accord took place gave them not a moment's pause. The voters were fools and must not be allowed to vote. Ho could have no legitimacy and they would see to it that he didn't. Diem agreed that the national vote that should have taken place in July 1956, should not happen. Instead a rigged referendum would be held that would give the Vietnamese only two choices: Emperor Bao Dai or Diem. Diem argued with his US advisers when they told him to announce (falsely) that he had achieved sixty to seventy per cent of the vote. Diem insisted on ninety-eight per cent. Both figures were fictitious but Diem wanted a landslide. As Stalin said, 'It's not the votes that count, but who counts the votes.'

Similar manipulations were reported in the election that handed power to Stump. Long before George W. Bush, mugging for the camera, said, 'You're either with us or you're against us,' Foster Dulles told Sukarno of Indonesia, 'America's policy is global. You must be on one side or the other. Neutralism is immoral.' Eventually, Sukarno's 'neutralism' led the Dulles brothers to launch a domestic version of the Bay of Pigs – 'Archipelago', they called it. Sukarno became another monster who had to be destroyed. They armed and trained a rebel army of ten thousand aimed at Sukarno's overthrow.

Stump knew nothing about all this and when he dropped a bomb on Afghanistan he didn't know about the rebel army the CIA had armed and trained there either. He only knew Afghanistan was where the 'bad guys' lived. His view of the world was like the plot of *High Noon* and the United States was always Gary Cooper. Being president was something that interferred with his golf and once he realised how much the voters despised him, he preferred golf and often despatched his stone-faced vice president to deal with things. He had his limitations but at least he wasn't a lightning rod for criticism and contempt. He lacked Stump's permanent case of foot in mouth disease – something Stump shared with George W. Bush, who, as a Democrat politician from Texas (Ann Richardson) said, was born with a 'silver foot in his mouth'.

Stump knew nothing of Patrice Lumumba's independence speech, given in front of King Baudoin of Belgium. With the cruelties of the Belgian emperor Leopold II burning in his brain, he was like a man on fire. The Belgians hadn't bothered to educate the Congolese: in 1960 there were just seventeen college graduates in a population of thirteen million. Lumumba was not one of them. He attended religious schools and did three years of high school. He was a voracious reader and passed a rigorous exam to become a postal clerk, a civil service job. He was a tireless campaigner and activist for Congolese independence, so he was in jail when the conference on independence took place. He had been shackled and his back was laced with wounds from floggings but the Belgians were forced to release him for the conference in Brussels. An election was held and Lumumba was suddenly prime minister of the Congo. It was in this capacity that he gave his speech, confident that independence was firmly in place. The speech marked him as what Stump would have considered an 'uppity nigger' and what the Dulles brothers would have considered a radical 'neutralist' and therefore a 'monster'. He was thirty-four, tall and thin with a goatee, and he wore glasses. He wanted an independent state, to regulate the exploitation of natural resources and to keep the Congo out of the Cold War. The fact that Congo was a rich source of uranium meant that the US would never let this happen. Worse still, the Congo was a source of industrial diamonds, copper, manganese, zinc, cobalt and chromium. The uranium used to create the bombs dropped on Hiroshima and Nagasaki came from the Congo.

'Our wounds are too fresh and too painful for us to drive them from our memory,' his speech began. 'We have known sarcasm and insults, endured blows morning, noon and night because we were niggers.' When Lumumba said that independence was not the gift of the Belgians, but a triumph of 'passionate and idealistic struggle' and that the Congo had thrown off 'the humiliating slavery that was imposed on it by force', King Baudoin was said to have turned deathly pale. Lumumba's speech was interrupted no less than eight times by wild cheering and applause. But the Belgians would have their revenge – two years later they executed Lumumba. With the help of the CIA, of course, and the invaluable assistance of the UN's blundering ambivalence.

And what did Stump know about Castro? Nothing useful. He wouldn't have known that America always regarded Cuba as a prospective additional state. Like Hawaii, it was seen as a candidate for annexation. Even when America granted Cuba limited self-rule, US troops still landed any time America felt its interests were threatened. The belief that they 'owned' Cuba only contributed to US outrage when Castro took it away from them – and from the Mafia. Stump would have found it equally outrageous, because to him America must always have what it wanted, just as he must always have what he wanted – whether it was a woman, a building or a deal. Stump would never have called those who blew up a ship in the harbour of Havana or burned down a department store, or burned sugar plantations, terrorists. Even though this was plainly anti-Castro terrorism. To Stump, terrorism could only happen to America – all these other things were what he would have called 'housekeeping' and when America carried out terrorism in the third world or when he ordered it, he saw it as 'self-defence'.

Allen Dulles was behind most of the anti-Castro terror which began soon after the Cuban Revolution. He never doubted that he would get Cuba back and so the Bay of Pigs fiasco moved forward under the control of Richard Bissell, put in charge by Dulles. The people put together to carry it out were the same people Dulles had used to overthrow Abenz in Guatemala. He had no reason to believe that the operation wouldn't be crowned with the same success. The arrogant petulance that was Stump's norm was America's norm too – which is why Stump ended up in the White House. That arrogant petulance was the hallmark of the Bay of Pigs invasion. Che Guevara told Castro that the CIA had succeeded in Guatemala for two reasons: Abenz had allowed an open society, which the CIA subverted for their own purposes, and Abenz had kept the existing army, which the CIA had used against Abenz. Castro would avoid these errors. He crushed dissent and purged the army. It was like a game of chess and Castro was brilliant at it. Castro recognised China and signed a trade deal with the USSR. Soviet petroleum arrived in Cuba and when the American oil companies refused to refine it, Castro nationalised those companies. When the US stopped buying Cuban sugar, he sold it to the Soviets.

This was intolerable and it would not be tolerated but in Castro Dulles had met his match. He just didn't know it yet. Eisenhower had approved plans to assassinate Castro – with the usual plausible deniability in place. For that task, Dulles hired the Mafia. One of Eisenhower's advisers suggested staging a false Cuban attack (standard false flag attack) on Guantanamo Bay as a pretext for war and invasion of Cuba. Mafia gangsters were handed six poison pills to use on Castro. It was like the plot of an Ealing comedy from the heyday of British cinema but everyone took it very seriously.

This lack of irony was another of Stump's norms. So there he was, flabby, florid, foolish and the leader of the free world. No doubt also somewhat shell-shocked at how little power a US president really has. Unless he wants to bomb a third world country. Then there is no end of support. The Bay of Pigs fiasco being a textbook example. Kennedy never wanted it but was assured by Allen Dulles that it could not fail. Secretly, the entire CIA believed that if it looked like failing, Kennedy could be blackmailed into making sure it didn't by sending planes to bomb Cuba. Kennedy had resolutely refused to do any such thing, so it was more wishful thinking than anything else. When former secretary of state, Dean Acheson, visited Kennedy at the White House he told him the CIA was going to invade Cuba. Acheson was astonished. 'Are you serious?' he said. 'It doesn't take Price Waterhouse to figure out that fifteen hundred Cubans are not as good as twenty-five thousand.' But once the wheels were in motion on a CIA covert operation, no amount of common sense can apply the brakes. It wasn't as if Kennedy had not made his position absolutely clear. The most pressure came from Admiral Arleigh Burke, who invaded the oval office 'late in the evening' to try to pin Kennedy down when it had become clear that the Bay of Pigs was a fiasco. The CIA's hardy band of ex-Cuban invaders had been hit with Castro's artillery, struck by Castro's bombers and set upon by Castro's troops. Those not killed were captured.

Burke: Let me take two jets and shoot down those enemy aircraft.

Kennedy: No. I don't want the US involved in this.

Burke: Can I not send in an air strike?

Kennedy: No.

Burke: Can I send in a few planes?

Kennedy: No. Because they would be identified as United States.

Burke: Can we paint out their numbers?

Kennedy: No.

Burke: Will you authorise artillery attacks on Cuban forces from American destroyers?

Kennedy: No.

That would be no, then. Kennedy told an aide later that day, 'I probably made a mistake keeping Dulles.' And that would be an understatement but one that probably led to Kennedy's own death. In fact, the salient point here is that Kennedy ended up dead and Dulles did not. Dulles ended up on the Warren Commission, which was allegedly trying to find out the truth about Kennedy's death. After the Bay of Pigs, which took place in April, Dulles only lasted until August, when Kennedy fired him. As for Dulles's activities on the Warren Commission, an observer summed them up thus: 'He systematically used his influence to keep the Commission safely within bounds, the importance of which only he could appreciate… From the start, before any evidence was reviewed he pressed for the final verdict that Oswald had been a crazed gunman, not the agent of a national or international conspiracy'. Kennedy's 'no' had been trumped by Dulles's fathomless deceit and his mania for overthrowing other countries' governments and his ability to create fiction out of fact.

But the task of creating someone like Stump, a character out of a comic book, as president of the United States would have stumped even Allen Dulles. A fact can be simply unbelievable, impossible to spin. Diego Rivera would have been up to the task. One can only imagine how Rivera would have depicted Stump in one of his murals but we know how he painted Allen Dulles and Foster Dulles. In his mural *Glorious Victory*,

Rivera depicted the CIA's overthrow of the Abenz government in Guatemala. John Foster Dulles is wearing a flak jacket and grinning. Allen stares with contempt, his chin resting on his brother's shoulder. A bag of money dangles from his waist. Eisenhower's face smiles from the side of a bomb in front of them. There are dead Guatemalan children lying at their feet. The background shows workers bent over under the weight of bags of bananas being loaded on to a ship flying the American flag.

Yes, Rivera could have captured Stump for posterity. He would have understood not only what he was, but what he meant. A critic once dismissed *Glorious Victory* as 'pure propaganda' and George Orwell wrote that 'All art is propaganda.' On the other hand, it's not propaganda when it's true.

True North

The book launch was at two p.m. the following Wednesday. A new poetry collection of mine called *True North* would be launched into the world. The title poem had been written about my husband. My third. I met him at a party. We ended up in bed and were rarely apart after that. I was already writing the poems that would become *True North*, but not with any urgency. I was writing a crime novel at the same time and that took most of my writing time. It was about a domestic monster and it was funny to be writing about a male monster while falling more and more in love with David – who was in every way the opposite of a male monster. He would bring me a cup of tea in bed each morning before he got dressed for work. He ran a coffee shop and bookstore in the city called Pepper's. Named after a dog he remembers from childhood. He was funny, kind and stoic: nothing made him feel sorry for himself. He took each challenge in life head on, wrestled it to the ground and, through sheer stubbornness, defeated it. He never gave up. So I should have realised that he wouldn't give me up either.

I could have held the book launch at Pepper's but that would have been too obvious and I went out of my way never to be obvious. So it was being held at Avid Reader, just down the road from Pepper's. It took a couple of years for the poetry collection to come together; poems were discarded, rewritten and finally collected into a file on my computer. I wrote while David was at work. I know they say the night belongs to the novelist but if I don't sleep, I go gaga, so I was a daytime writer. I would write until the words were blurry on the page and around four p.m. I would think about dinner and wash up. Never been able to write on a computer. Don't know why. The computer is for editing and for emailing the finished product to the publisher.

At first I didn't know how much he was influencing the poems. I had no plan. I wasn't proceeding from a theme; there was no particular thing I wanted to say. Even when I wrote things like this, I had no idea he was my theme:

Skin

Such skin he has.
So fine, so tanned,
so warm.
It cradles me and buries me…

Of course it can be a mistake to make someone you're in love with your theme. It's a perilous path. But since I couldn't see the forest for the trees, the peril was not obvious. Each poem seemed to be 'about' something different, and it only became obvious to me when the collection was read as a whole that this was essentially a collection of love poems. And somehow he had set me free. I always felt that there was a wall between me and what I was writing but now the wall was gone. That was even more obvious in the novel I was writing than the poetry. Since I met David, I had somehow broken through to another level. One I never expected to reach. From the opening line, this novel was different: 'I always thought of my mother as a soldier. A conscript in someone else's war,' it began. Some days, the novel just wrote itself and all I could do was hang on to the pen and put it down on the page. I wrote the novel with my head and the poems with my heart.

One day, after writing the gruelling and bloody incident where the protagonist of my novel, Bill Morrison, beats his wife into a hospital bed, I needed to go to another place. I turned to the notebook where I was writing the poetry collection and this is what I wrote:

Red

The red of love
is the tip of a flame.
Not like the red of war
with its bloodied corpses,
bombs, noise and grief.

Not like the red of hate.
The distorted face,
the bulging veins,
the clenched fists.

Not the red of cruelty.
Not the red of shame.
It is the red of the hibiscus,
the red of wine,
the red of a sun at sunset.
It is the scarlet that burns your eyes.

As Omar Khayyam wrote:
The day on which you are
without passionate love
is the most wasted day of your life.

 I wasn't planning to marry David. After two failures, I didn't want another one. And I thought we would eventually go our separate ways – none of my relationships had lasted. I thought he thought that too. But he was very observant. He looked at the two books I had written when I was with my former husbands and wheels turned in his head.

 I didn't know this, but I remember he asked me once after dinner, 'Did you break up with both your husbands after you finished a book?'

 'Yes,' I told him. I didn't know that this had caused him to reflect deeply.

 The novel had escaped. This is always a good sign. I found myself with a daughter now plotting her father's murder. This had not been part of my plan but when I started writing it down it all felt so right that I just went with it. I was already writing the novel when I met David but when he moved in with me, it really took flight. Clearly he was good for my writing but, as the poetry collection came together and the novel grew chapter by chapter, I got careless. My mouth has always been my downfall in relationships.

 One morning, I told him I was going for a walk. He wanted to come with me. I wanted to go alone. He became a bit agitated, but nothing major – or so I thought.

'No,' I told him. 'I want to work out the ending of a poem.'
'Can't you do it here?' he said.
'No, I need to clear my head.'
He looked at me in a funny way.
'What's wrong?'
'Why can't I come?' he said, quietly.
'I need to think. I need to think about the ending in my head. For that, I need to be alone.'

I thought this was perfectly reasonable and he seemed to accept it. He gave me another funny look but he walked to the door with me and gave me a peck on the cheek, so I thought everything was fine. I drove to a nearby walking track and went for a bushwalk. The fresh air cleared my head and I worked out the ending for the poem. It was not going to be in *True North* but was in a notebook in which I was writing new poems. This is the poem with the new ending.

Collision

The words crash and burn;
nothing scans.
I cross them out.
Put them in coffins.

I know the words
will eventually do what I want.
I just have to wait on the muse.

So I put the notebook aside.
Drink coffee.
Listen to Neil Young and Crowded House.
Put food out for the birds.

I wait,
humming,
like a car that wants to race.
Wait for the moment
when I can dip the pen
in my veins,
write with the blood.

When I got back to the house, David was sitting at the kitchen table and there was anger in the air. I approached carefully.

'I hope I'm not going to join the queue,' he said, darkly, stirring sugar into his coffee.

'What queue?' I said in all innocence. I thought I caught a whiff of alcohol as I got closer to him. 'Are you drinking this early in the day?' I asked, once again in all innocence. I even laughed a bit.

He rose from the table, drew himself up to his full height, loomed over me. 'Why did you really want to go on your own?' he said, in the same dark tone.

'Oh, David!' I said impatiently. 'What do you think I was doing? Meeting my lover?'

At that, he threw his coffee cup and coffee went all over the wall. The cup smashed. This was one of those make or break moments I suddenly realised. It was like when a storm blows up out of a clear blue sky.

'What are you doing?' I demanded. 'Why did you do that?'

'I've worked it out,' he said. 'You use people as material for your books. Once the book is done, you keep the book and get rid of the person. Well, you're not throwing me away. I won't let you. Either you marry me or we're finished.'

This last was said with absolute finality. It was not a negotiation, it was a statement of fact. The fierce emotion shocked me. He wasn't normally like this. He was always so reasonable and so calm.

I moved towards him but he backed away.

'I need an answer,' he said. 'I need to know where I stand.'

It was clear to me that he saw the publication of the book as a danger. He seemed to believe that we would now break up because my two former husbands had gone after a book was published. That it was pure coincidence would not be accepted by him in his current mood. He wouldn't let me touch him; he just stood there waiting for my answer.

'Well, that's not the most romantic proposal,' I told him. 'But if you want to marry me so much, then we'll get married.'

Very soon after, we were married. I couldn't really follow his line of thought on this. Because, if my two other marriages had ended because I had published a book, what was to stop it happening again? Being married did seem to make him more secure, though, and I admired his stubbornness and his determination to make me commit to him. *True North* was written because of that. I wanted to praise his constancy and his unwavering adherence to what he believed in. The word 'true' being the important one in this poem.

True North

Iron clings to a magnet.
Metal filings fly through air
to embrace it.
So I cling to you and fly to you.
Forces that I don't understand draw me.
I who love freedom,
have none.

To find my way,
I must know the difference
between magnetic north and true north.
True north is aligned to the North Pole
and is constant.
Something to believe in when
all the gods have failed,
or gone away.

West – watch the sunset
and you're facing west.
South – face the sun at midday
and you are facing south.
East – standing at dawn facing
the rising sun you are looking east.
North – point to the left,
while watching the sun rise
and you are pointing north.

There's a scientific reason,
I'm sure,
for why I turn in your direction.

> Why I orbit you like a moon.
> North, east, south and west all lead to you.
> So there is no difference,
> whatever the compass says.
>
> But the compass prevents shipwreck,
> and there have I been, too often.
> True north, the other north, is essential
> for navigation.
> For a precise line that takes you
> where you want to go.
>
> While love is a mystery that lies,
> even to itself,
> true north is as true as any fact.
> Truer than most.
> And constant.
> The fidelity of its calculation
> is unwavering.
> While that of the human heart is fatally fickle,
> and only true to itself.

The book launch was a big success. A poet who was a university lecturer and taught creative writing launched the book, praising my 'poet's eye' and my 'empathy'. David was sitting in the audience when I did my reading of 'True North'. If he thought it was about him, he gave no sign. Later, when all the books were sold and the floor was covered in paper cups and cake crumbs and everyone was gone, David and I sipped champagne and looked at the city lights, twinkling in the dark outside. We toasted the book.

'I liked the one about the compass,' he said.

'The one about you, you mean?' I teased.

'Was it about me?'

'Yes.'

'Oh, I didn't get that,' he said, looking nonplussed.

'The connection is a bit obscure,' I told him.

The woman who owned the bookstore suddenly appeared. 'I've come to lock up,' she said. 'I think it went very well. We have some orders for the book from people who missed out on a copy.'

'Good work,' I told her, pouring her a glass of champagne.

Then David and I walked out into the velvety night, the inky sky so clear you felt you could reach up and take a star as a souvenir. If the future was written in the stars, they weren't telling me anything that night. I would just have to wait and see what happened, like everyone else.

The Eye Out of a Needle

My mother beat me for stealing. So did my father. It had no effect. Stealing wasn't my vice: it was my vocation. Nothing could make me give it up. A definition of kleptomania is 'an irresistible impulse to steal stemming from emotional disturbance rather than economic need'. But in fact, sometimes it *was* economic need: most times it wasn't. Generally, I stole things I didn't strictly need – in the sense that I never stole food or medicine. Sometimes I did it just to liven up a dull day. From time to time, I looked up the symptoms of kleptomania:

1. Inability to resist powerful urges to steal items that you don't need.
2. Feeling increased tension, anxiety or arousal leading up to the theft.
3. Feeling pleasure, relief or gratification while stealing.

Then I compared them to my own experience. Sometimes I laughed at myself for doing it but it gave me no joy at all to know my 'illness' was classified as a mental illness. The first thing I remember stealing belonged to my mother. I was nine. A brooch she particularly liked. I stole it out of her jewellery box and hid it under my mattress. She mentioned it several times over the next few days but I felt no remorse. I never felt remorse about anything I stole. I had vague feelings of superiority but no regrets. It was always a thrill to get away with it. My mother seemed to become more obsessed with the missing brooch with each passing day but it never occurred to me to put it back. Once I had taken something, it was mine. This seemed to me to be an irrefutable fact. I never questioned it or the logic of it. If I was clever enough to steal something, I had earned it.

'Amanda, you haven't seen that brooch of mine, have you? The green one?' my mother asked me one day.

'No.'

'I can't understand where it's gone,' she said while she distractedly stirred some porridge on the stove.

'I haven't seen it,' I lied.

'It was my mother's,' she said.

And now it's mine, I thought.

I never gave it back. It was under my mattress for years. Until I left home, in fact. By which time, my mother was dead. I took the brooch with me when I left. I never gave anything back.

At fifteen I was working in a grocery store, having persuaded my mother to let me leave school. I stole from morning until night. Pantyhose, hand cream and a lot of useless junk I didn't need and couldn't use. All crammed in my handbag and put away behind a curtain on a cupboard in the shop. I also stole money, of course. Once I had perfected the trick of silencing the bell on the side of the cash register so that I could open it undetected, there was no stopping me. I knew so little about such things as balancing a cash register and bookkeeping that the fact that the discrepancy would be obvious to the shop owners was lost on me.

Eventually, the day came when I was confronted, accused and ordered from the shop. My mother and father were devastated. My mother told me tearfully that she had never stolen so much as a pin in her life – which was no doubt true, but beside the point: she was not a thief, but I was.

Later, I became much more sophisticated at hiding my thefts. I learned from the debacle in the grocery store that stealing was an art and I had better master it or I would end up permanently unemployed or in jail. The shop owners did not involve the police. I was only fifteen and they weren't prepared to, as they saw it, ruin my life. Instead, I was bundled off back to school, where I completed my junior certificate with very respectable marks. I was not cured of stealing. There was no cure for what ailed me – whatever it was.

I decided the best way to legitimise my stealing was to become an accountant – so that's what I did. I did bookkeeping in my junior year at school and got a good mark for it. Then I did a degree in accounting at university. I learned how to make money disappear by moving it from one side of the ledger to the other. I learned how to steal money and leave no trace of the theft. I was able to indulge my illness and earn a very good living at the same time. It was the perfect occupation for me. Other thefts were not so easy to cover up but I led a charmed life in that regard. Even if I was found out, there was never enough evidence to do anything about it. The police were never involved. I was young, female, had a respectable profession and no one dared move against me – even if they knew I was a thief. Either that or one of the fallen angels had been given the job of looking after me.

It was always so easy. People trusted me. Any group I joined always put me in a position of responsibility sooner or later. The tennis club I joined was no exception. They made me treasurer – with predictable results. I always meant to bank all of the money that was being saved in a bank account for the end of year tennis Christmas bash but somehow some of it (small amounts in themselves) always stuck to my fingers. I told myself I would pay it in later, but of course I never did. As ever, once I had stolen something, it was mine.

Since I never paid it back into the bank account, sooner or later the theft would come to light. And so it did. About two weeks before Christmas, the money was finally needed to pay for dinner in a nice restaurant. But the amount of money in the account was far less than was required for the members of a tennis club to go and have a nice meal in a nice restaurant. The only way it could have happened was if someone, namely me, had taken it. But most of them still didn't dare confront me. Only one of them decided to grill me about the money. She was an attractive woman, married to an engineer. She had glossy, straight black hair, very white teeth and blue eyes as cold as ice. She bowled up to me and confronted me. Asked straight out what had happened to the money. I said nothing. What could I say? Silence was the safest option. She skewered me with a furious look of contempt then turned on her heel and walked away.

Once again, I felt no shame and no remorse. I felt superior. I had fooled them and they couldn't lay a hand on me. They couldn't prove a thing because I had always taken the money as cash before I banked it. There was no money trail and no proof either way. But they all knew. I went to the (budget) meal in the restaurant mostly so I could enjoy their discomfort. Which I did. No one could make eye contact with me and inside I was laughing my head off. I left the club soon after.

Jean Genet wrote in T*he Thief's Journal* that the boldness of a thief's life was what excited him. You can be humiliated in many ways. Genet describes being humiliated in *The Thief's Journal* by the police who had arrested him. They found a tube of Vaseline in his pocket which had mentholatum in it. 'You take it up the nose?' they jeered, reeking of garlic and writhing with laughter. It was already obvious that he was gay but as well as that he was a beggar and a thief – an object of absolute contempt, in other words, and the little tube of Vaseline sealed the bargain.

I never faced any humiliation because I was a thief. I was too clever and too affluent to be caught. Or so I told myself. But then there is that saying: 'Set a thief to catch a thief.' Not that he intended to catch me in that sense. In the sense of catching me as the rooster catches the hen, he was right on target. His intentions from the start were to enchant me and bed me – both of which he did. He wore a black vest, black pants and a white shirt when I first saw him in a crowded pub. He had longish jet-black hair and a gold earring in one ear. He was picking pockets left, right and centre with a skill that took most of my breath away. He wore his beauty with a casual air, as if it didn't much matter to him, as if he didn't value it. When he approached me, I gave him a collegial smile: the kind a worker might give a co-worker. Were we not in the same trade?

His name was Cary Williams. The minute he told me his name, I was mesmerised. As if I had been waiting to hear that name all my life. When we went to bed, we had sex all night. He woke me every three hours – like a breast feeding baby. I was shivery and breathless and any way he touched me gave me pleasure. It was hard to leave him the next morning in his messy flat that reeked of cigarettes and alcohol and go back to my accountancy and my kleptomania. He gave me his phone number and a lopsided grin. I gave him my number too.

'Call me, yeah?' he said.

I left and walked down the street to find a cab. I didn't think I would be with him again, which was a pity, but I wasn't the kind to give in to melancholy. There were too many things to steal for me to ever completely despair. But I was wrong about not being with him again anyway, as it turned out.

We fell into a pattern.

He would phone around six p.m. and say, 'Should I pick you up?'

I would say, 'Yes.'

He would pick me up in his beaten-up Honda and we would go to his flat. Sometimes we ate pizza. I hate pizza but I loved eating pizza with him. Then we would go to bed and he would make me happy all night long. I wasn't used to being happy and feeling that way made me realise that I had been unhappy most of my life. He was a thief but not a clever one like me. I didn't think that mattered but in the end it did.

Very soon, I was in love with him, lived for the sound of 'Stupid Girl' playing on my mobile phone, knowing he was at the other end of the line. He only ever rang once a week – I never knew what day it would be but it was often a Friday – and for him I was sure it was just pure sex with no emotions involved. But I was wrong about that too. For the first three months, we never went out, only to bed and I thought we were very cool, wayward and Bohemian, which in a way we were, but there's always more to everything than meets the eye.

Opening a cupboard next to his bed one morning, I found it was full of wallets. They all still had the ID of the owners in them and their photographs but no cash and no cash cards or Visa cards. I looked at their various faces in the licence photos. I didn't feel sorry for them but I was a bit disappointed in Cary's lack of vision. There was so much more he could do.

He was my diligent student in scams as I was his diligent student in bed. We taught each other a lot. I began his tuition with the Spanish Lotto Scam. Letters addressed to individuals purporting to inform them of a lottery win in Spain are part of this cunning con job. There are variations on the theme, but many such letters request the recipient to pass over their bank account details. More commonly, the intended victim is asked to contact a number in Spain (a mobile phone represented by nine digits starting with a 6) to claim their prize. Once contact is made, they are told that certain fees need to be paid in advance. The victim is then typically strung along with ever more taxes and other charges which need to be paid before the prize can be theirs.

The scam is similar to those which operate in many parts of the world. However, the Spanish scams refer to what are indeed legitimate lotteries in Spain, for example El Gordo and La Primitiva. Spain's biggest lottery, El Gordo (literally 'the fat one'), is drawn every year on 22 December. Lottery tickets do not go on sale via official lottery offices until August of each year and are sold only in Spain. Only the Spanish National Mint issues official lottery tickets and, when purchased, the tickets are not registered in the purchaser's name or address. Prize money can only be obtained upon the presentation of the winning ticket at an official lottery office in Spain, or via a bank which has a registered branch in Spain, within three months of the draw.

Many people had lost large sums of money because they fell for this scam and once I explained the sheer simplicity of it to Cary, he saw at once that it was genius. The genius scams are always based on a simple premise – that human beings will always believe they can get something for nothing, in spite of bountiful evidence to the contrary. There are people who do actually get something for nothing but they fall into two categories: those who were born into privilege and thieves. Neither Cary nor I fitted the description of 'born into privilege' but neither, in most cases, did our marks. Working with Cary would give me the feeling of superiority I craved, so I thought. I had no remorse in the planning or the execution. No interest in the fact that we would be taking people's life savings. Cary had no interest in that either. We were a perfect match.

After he had mastered the Spanish Lotto Scam, we moved on to the Pigeon Drop. It was relatively simple and relied on human gullibility in the same way but it had a lot more moving parts and was harder to teach:

but Cary was sharp, a quick study, and he soon mastered it too. The Pigeon Drop revolved around a fiction: that those running the scam had found a large sum of money, say $70,000, usually in a bag in a parking lot. There would be a note in the bag detailing the history of the money: that it had been won at the racetrack, for example. The story then evolved. The scammer and the mark could keep the money but exactly how much the scammer and the mark could keep would be decided by an equally fictitious 'boss' who would allegedly be consulted in his 'office' while the mark waited in the car. Then the scammer would come back to the car and tell the mark that they could keep a large sum of money, say $20,000 each. But first the mark must make a 'good faith' payment of $5,000. At this point, it all depended on the skill of the scammer, but if all went well and the mark was hooked, they would be driven to the bank to withdraw this sum – which would in many cases be their life savings.

Now Cary was ready to work and make lots of money. More than he had ever made picking pockets and stealing wallets. For me, it was kleptomania by proxy because I didn't intend to take any of the money he made.

I enjoyed the descriptions Jean Genet put in *The Thief's Journal* of shoplifting in department stores. He described in full, for example, how a shoplifter could stand in front of piles of silk remnants and put one hand into the pocket of an overcoat, a pocket which had been slit. Then the thief moves right up to the counter until their stomach is touching it and pulls the silk remnant into the pocket through the slit. Some of his descriptions of stealing are almost poetic. When he describes another thief's technique, which he calls 'science' and 'like military science', he also describes the stolen products as 'falling stars' that streamed in a 'pure, brief curve' into the thief's trousers, seeming to swell his thighs.

I couldn't resist putting these things into practice and on many Friday nights we went on stealing sprees where we stole everything from boxes of chocolates and bottles of wine to teacups and lingerie. It was like foreplay. With the stolen loot in the boot of the Honda, we would drive back to his flat in triumph. He would feed me chocolates as we lay naked in bed. We would drink the wine and then I would model the lingerie for him, until he removed it before making love to me.

If only we had stopped there. But my feelings of superiority, my fatal arrogance, now knew no bounds and I couldn't wait to get Cary started on the scams. I longed to see my apprentice and proxy in action.

His first mark was a schoolteacher. This made the whole thing even more delicious. That someone who most people would consider, on the face of it, to be a moderately intelligent person fell for the Pigeon Drop was something Cary thought was quite a feather in his cap. He left her at the so-called 'office', sent her in to talk to the 'boss' – who of course didn't exist. While she searched in vain for the boss and the non-existent office, Cary made his escape – with $7,000 of her hard-earned cash.

He had a reckless streak that only added to his charm as a love object but was not ideal for someone involved in scams. He began scamming on an epic scale and no amount of warnings from me had any effect. He had plastic bags of money all over his flat, hidden in various places, some even under the floorboards and in the freezer.

'We'll go to Europe and live like kings' was one of his favourite expressions at this time. He had always had this fantasy, he told me, and was determined to put together a couple of million dollars to make it a reality, but he was an amateur and it often showed. Sometimes he phoned someone he was scamming with the Pigeon Drop and mistakenly began talking about their winnings in the Spanish lottery. He was clever enough to get himself out of such scrapes but how long could his mistakes not bring his house of cards crashing down?

'You need to cool it,' I told him. 'Slow down.'

But he never listened. He was money-mad at this point. Could see us in the south of France driving a convertible, tanned and free.

'Open some bank accounts and bank that money. You need at least ten accounts,' I scolded but he took no notice. The idea that suddenly banking huge amounts of money would be very conspicuous and bring unwanted attention was lost on him.

In the end, I had to open the accounts, when I had not wanted to be involved, while driving around with numerous plastic bags of money in the boot of my car. All very risky.

When I complained, he just shrugged, gave me the lopsided grin and said, 'Come to bed.'

I did. I couldn't resist him and he couldn't resist money and theft.

Then, fatefully, he encountered an obstreperous, middle-aged woman with a rich husband and lots of money to throw around. But of course even the rich always want more and believe they can get something for nothing. She would bring him down, but there was no way he could have known that. He was not experienced in reading marks: I would never have gone near her. She was trouble. I would have smelled it, but all Cary could smell was money. He tried the Pigeon Drop on her and she seemed to have fallen for it – but nothing could have been further from the truth. While he was envisaging all the money he could take her for, she was at home with her rich husband telling him she knew it was a scam and that they should contact the police. In due course, they did.

Genet says in *The Thief's Journal* that 'thieving is a form of betrayal' and I was to drink the bitter cup of betrayal and drain the dregs. I would come to know exactly what Shakespeare meant when he wrote, 'How sharper than a serpent's tooth is an ungrateful child.' Though Cary was not my child, the pain was what mattered and it was the same as the serpent's tooth sinking into flesh and injecting poison.

When they arrested Cary, he was completely amazed. As amazed as if aliens had landed a spacecraft on his balcony. Being arrested had never figured in his plans but he had been in jail, briefly, before and he was terrified of going back there. They searched his flat and found all the plastic bags of money that I had not yet banked. The woman had phoned him and made plans to meet him and like a fool he gave her his address. The police were with her when she phoned: very determined to put a scammer out of action. Cary denied everything. The plastic bags weren't his. They belonged to a friend. He was just looking after them for said friend. He knew nothing about any scams. But, of course, they pressed him. Who was the friend? Did he have no suspicions when he saw all that money? Where did he think it came from? Backed into a corner, Cary lied until he was exhausted but the questions kept coming and he kept tripping over the previous lies. As liars do.

They questioned him for hours, while observing all the rules, because they were determined to nail him – even though they suspected he was the accomplice and the puppet master was someone else. They were prepared to believe his story, they told him, if he gave them the name of the mastermind – and that would of course be me. He held out manfully for a long time but then he thought about going back to jail and he began to sweat. Sweat was dripping off him, off his forehead especially, and getting in his eyes, blinding him. He began to panic. The cops knew he was about to crack, they had seen it all before, so they poured the pressure on relentlessly. And he did crack. I'm sure he remembered our trysts and what he called my strawberries and cream breasts, and remembered them fondly. But he also remembered his last stint in jail for break and enter. Exhausted and panicky and with tears in his eyes he ratted on me. 'I want to make a statement,' he said.

I knew nothing of this until the police arrived at my house to arrest me. I was as amazed as Cary had been. To see the burly policemen at my door was startling but also oddly exciting. I suppose I had always known it would come to this, deep down inside. Being in love with Cary had made me reckless – as reckless as he was. But I had blinded myself to all of that and now those chickens had come home to roost.

Cary got a suspended sentence because of his cooperation with the police. I got four years, eligible for release in two.

When I was released, I asked around and heard through the grapevine that Cary had gone back to New Zealand. He had ratted and run: the shine was coming off him more and more but I still had a sweet feeling in my blood whenever I said his name. I wasn't cured of my kleptomania either. My so-called illness burned brighter than ever. I was a thief and I always would be and for all I knew it was genetic or some kind of personality disorder. I knew personality disorders were incurable. I would have given all the money in the world for just one hour in Cary's bed in his dingy flat, but I told myself there are dreams that can't come true. I was now substituting stealing for that pleasure, as I had in some sense substituted it for my life.

At a loose end, I joined a book club. They made me treasurer and I started saving money for the end of the year Christmas party. I had a bad case of déjà vu. I stole at least half the money but it didn't matter now. I could easily put it back. Cary had been loyal in one way: he had told the police nothing about the bank accounts that I had so carefully set up in ways that could not be detected by the police. All that money was now mine. I didn't need to work, so I didn't. I told myself, without much real conviction, that I was still lucky because I was affluent and not in jail. And I was still able to practise my true vocation: thieving. But Cary had smashed a hole in my heart that no amount of thieving would fill. I would always be the walking wounded now. My conviction that I was smarter than everyone else was in tatters too. Of course I would go on stealing – I had to – but the glory days of stealing wine and chocolates with Cary were just a beautiful memory.

Sitting in a coffee shop, I noticed a woman staring at me and I realised that I knew her. It was the engineer's wife from the tennis club, the one who had confronted me over the money I had stolen as their treasurer. She was with two other women. She said something to them and they all laughed. My case had been in the paper, so she knew all about it. I felt no shame, defiantly refused to feel it. I thought, 'I have experienced things you will never know, you poor thing,' as I studied her gleaming white teeth and her straight, gleaming black hair. I drank my coffee and ignored her and the two women she was with when they made a point of walking past me on their way out.

Cary had written me a letter which I had read only the day before. In it, he expressed his sorrow that he had betrayed me and asked me to call him, including his mobile phone number. I wouldn't call him. Not yet. It could even be a trap, I decided. I would ignore it for the time being. But it wouldn't be completely out of the question for me to go to New

Zealand at some point and see if he still lived at the address on the back of the envelope. He deserved to have at least some of the money he had worked so hard to accumulate via those scams. Even if he didn't make it to the south of France, some of that money would make his life easier. Of course, I knew how easily we could start squabbling over the money because there is, as the saying goes, no honour among thieves. I wrote the address on the back of the envelope into my pocket address book and put it back in my purse.

I was on my way to a department store to try out some of the tricks Genet had so generously shared in *The Thief's Journal*. Walking out the door of the coffee shop, I remembered something that Genet wrote about one of his lovers, describing his impertinent smile as he watched Genet adore him. Then I remembered Cary's dark eyes watching me as I kissed his pale, slim body; the wide grin and his sardonic, pink mouth as he contemplated my helpless adoration. Straight or gay, some things are always the same.

Rome, Twice

1980

We went to Rome on a whim. I had seen *Gidget Goes to Rome* but that was hardly preparation. Coming in over Italy on the Lufthansa jet, I saw a lot of unbelievably green fields below me. Coming in over Sydney, the first thing you see is red roofs. Coming in over Hamburg is much the same: red roofs and red-brick buildings amongst a lot of grey concrete blocks of flats. But my first sight of Italy was just an impression of incredibly green squares and rectangles with funny little fences. When I went to see *Heaven*, the Tommy Twyker film, the aerial shots of Italy reminded me of flying towards Rome.

Out of the airport and into the city, where we found a place to stay. A big room and a big bed in a pension located in a narrow cobblestoned street. There were a lot of these streets and they all looked the same, so on at least one occasion we walked in ever more desperate circles until the found our hotel. When I'd asked him if he was lost, my husband looked stoic and plodded on. He will never admit to being lost. He thinks it's unmanly.

Next day outside the railway station, I saw a beautiful, dark-haired boy of about seven, standing near the station wall. He was wearing a brown, belted coat and a pair of tiny shorts and brown shoes and ankle socks. His small, rather dirty hand was extended. He was a beggar. I stared with shock. I had never seen a child begging in my life until then. I had vivid memories of the coloured plate in my grade three reader of the Little Match Girl, who froze to death barefoot in the snow while more fortunate children ate their Christmas dinner.

I wanted to give the beggar boy some money but my husband said, 'No, his parents should send him to school.'

In the same situation again, I would give him the money. I've never forgotten walking past and the boy's placid brown eyes watching me.

Even in the ritzy outdoor cafés, grubby-looking women could be seen walking among the diners with their hands outstretched. I noticed the quick steps they took. It was similar to the way a stray dog walks: as if expecting something to be thrown at it, or to be kicked. The beggar women looked straight ahead; their hands moved from side to side. There are probably so many homeless people in Europe now that I suppose no one even bothers to count them.

Over a meal in a restaurant, my husband was talking about the Popemobile, the armour-plated car in which the Pope was driven around Rome for public appearances. I thought about what the Popemobile must have cost. My husband was saying it was bulletproof. Yes, it would have to be. I was thinking about how the Pope wants more children to be born into this overpopulated world and how he deplores all forms of contraception except the one that doesn't work. Even if children are born to be dumped on the streets to fend for themselves. Even if they form gangs and become criminals and prostitutes as they do in Latin America and are culled every so often like animals by the police of Latin America. We didn't see the Pope in his Popemobile, which was probably just as well, all things considered.

We did see the Coliseum, though. It was inhabited by thousands of cats and I felt the absolute horror of the place pressing in on me. It was like some frenzied chant in my head dying away, syllable by syllable – blood and sandals, blood and sand, blood… Humans beings were dismembered here, I was thinking. Unfortunately, I'm not a flippant traveller. Seeing my pale, haunted face, my husband suggested lunch. We travelled to the restaurant in a horse-drawn carriage and I threw coins in the Trevi Fountain. In spite of the legend that doing this meant I would return to Rome, I had never been back. I must still have been brooding on the Coliseum because somehow I managed to lock myself in the toilet. It was a Chinese restaurant and when I knocked and yelled and knocked and yelled, a team of waiters milled around outside the door speaking

Chinese. Finally one of them poked the key out of the keyhole onto a piece of newspaper and pulled it out to the other side of the door. I got the impression that this had happened many times before and they were too cheap to fix the lock. Freed, I went back to my table in a fit of pique and spilled my Chinese soup.

'Where's your umbrella?' my husband said, mopping up the soup with a serviette.

I had left it in the horse-drawn carriage.

'We shouldn't have gone to the Coliseum,' I told him, sulking.

He gave me an exasperated look and called for the bill.

Ruth Cracknell, in *Journey from Venice*, describes her discovery (brought about by her husband's serious illness while staying there) that underneath the glamour, Venice is a city that's still mediaeval. Rome's not mediaeval: it's older than time. I liked the Romans, liked the ambience, but I knew deep down that Rome doesn't care about people. It has drunk blood and tasted imperial glory and the glory that was Rome was not its people. The Coliseum is just a ruined amphitheatre but it was the Coliseum I remembered. To me, it was the true face of Rome, watching the beggars with the same indifference it had showed the Christian martyrs and the gladiators.

In a little shop in Rome, my husband had bought me a gift: a small piece of ivory, hooded in gold and carved in the shape of an animal's fang. It dangled from a gold chain as I looked down and saw the green fields of Italy receding under our plane on our way back to Australia. It seemed fitting somehow.

2017

I'm a widow now. The freedom is worse than the grief. Leaves you dizzy and feeling as if you're lost in space. The grief drags you down into the shadows, like a crocodile with its prey. And there you will stay unless you struggle to free yourself from its clutches. That was how I came to go to Rome again. I drifted for months, eighteen in all, and then my friends told me it was time to get on with life. They weren't being unkind, just truthful.

I decided to go to Rome because I had liked it the best of all the places I had been in Europe with my husband. I had a thing about art – my husband called it my affliction. He was a tradesman, which is why we were quite comfortable financially. He was never out of work. We had no children and there was a time in my thirties when I grieved over that too. But I came to see it as something that was meant to be and later I knew that if we had had children, they would have come between us – my attention would have shifted to them. I had seen other people I knew, friends and family, brought to the brink of emotional devastation by their children. I had seen marriages break up over the consequences of children's behaviour and crises. My job in the local library kept me busy and I was surrounded by books all day and since I loved books, I loved my job. My husband and I had a very pleasant life together, a life that had begun with passion and became over the years something essential to both of us, and I was in no way prepared for his death, which is silly really. But I had never even considered what I would do if he died. He was always so vigorous, so healthy. It was a shock when he died of a heart attack and the hole it left in my life was vast.

But now, slowly healing, I was planning my trip to Rome: I intended to see all of the galleries I had missed out on when I was in Rome first time round – and that was all of them because, as the French so wisely say, youth is wasted on the young. I was more interested in rock music than art the first time around. I went to the shelves in the library where I worked to find guides to most of the capital cities in the world and found one on Rome. Each lunch hour, I would sit in the staff room with my coffee and the Lonely Planet guide. All those palazzi stuffed with works of art made me almost salivate: Galleria Borghese, Galleria Nazionale d'Arte Antica… I wanted to see everything but one of my work colleagues, a well-travelled single woman, told me I would die of exhaustion if I tried to see everything. There was just too much to see – I had to whittle it down and only do one gallery every second day and use the alternate days to rest. 'Those palazzi are huge,' she warned me. I knew what she meant. I wasn't twenty-two this time round.

At the very least, I promised myself a feast of Caravaggio – *Narcissus, Boy Bitten by a Lizard*. They were in the Antica in Rome. I also had a fascination for Napoleon and I was excited to see that there was an entire museum dedicated to the Corsican. The Museo Napoleonico, it was called, and admission was free. A book I took in my luggage was *Midnight in Sicily*, by an Australian, Peter Robb. I had found it in a second-hand bookshop. Someone had cut out newspaper clippings and put them in the back of the book. They all dealt with the trial of Andreotti, former Mafia prime minister of Italy, and the activities of Silvio Berlusconi. I thought it would come in handy on the long plane trip but, as it turned out, it was to colour and influence my entire time in Rome.

My hotel was in the centre of Rome and I planned to get trains or buses to all of the museums and galleries I wanted to visit. My research on the internet also turned up an essay written on the murder of Italian director Pier Paolo Pasolini. He was killed the day before the premiere of *Salo*, his highly controversial film in which four fascists kidnap eigheen teenagers and subject them to endless rape and torture. This would also haunt my two weeks in Rome, if only as part of the atmospherics.

The flight was uneventful and I slept for much of it because it was a night flight. There was a stopover in Hong Kong, where I wandered, bleary-eyed, and tried to drink coffee. I bought some perfume, Chanel No. 5, out of sheer boredom. Then on to another plane and more sleep until arrival at Rome airport. Collecting my luggage seemed to take hours. I took a cab to the hotel rather than the train because I felt a bit ill and out of it, but put it down to the long flight. At the four-star hotel I had booked (no need to be extravagant), I abandoned my unpacked suitcase just inside the door, closed the door and fell on to the bed, where I slept for twelve hours. When I woke, it was midday and I was so sick I could barely focus on the clock on the wall. I decided I needed a doctor, so I phoned room service. There was a hotel doctor and he would be sent to my room. No sooner had I hung up than I had to rush to the bathroom to vomit. This was not part of my plan. How dare my body let me down like this?

The doctor was a handsome, olive-skinned man with white hair. 'It's a virus,' he said. 'You must rest, drink fluids and take painkillers for the pain.'

'I don't have any pain,' I told him in a weak voice I hardly recognised as my own.

'You will,' he said with a smile. 'Normally it starts with a headache and then the entire body aches. Take two of these every four hours but don't exceed eight in twenty-four hours. A virus usually lasts a week.'

A week! This couldn't be happening.

'You must rest,' he repeated. 'If you don't, you will get really sick. Best not to go out and be in crowds, spreading it around.'

He made it sound like bubonic plague. His English was excellent but what he was telling me made tears fill my eyes.

He put the painkillers on the bedside table next to a beautiful glass lamp. 'They will also keep your temperature down,' he said.

'I don't have a temperature,' I told him.

'You will.' He smiled again. 'Any concerns you have, ring room service and I will come back again. Drink lots of water,' he added, as he made his way to the door and disappeared.

I took the two painkillers he had left out for me with water from a glass jug I found in the refrigerator in the kitchen. I had booked an apartment wanting to do some Italian cooking myself but now I was too weak to cook anything and would have to rely on room service to survive, given the remote possibility that I would ever want to eat again. The vomiting, the dottore told me, was being caused by my temperature, the one I told him I didn't have, and once it came down I would feel much better. I put my hand on my forehead and realised I was bathed in sweat. Who was I kidding? I realised I had a raging fever. Antibiotics would do no good, the dottore told me, not with a virus.

So that was that. I had seven days of illness ahead of me and there was nothing I could do about it. The Museo Napoleonica was now a dream – it was all I could do to get into the bathroom to go to the toilet, to shower and to find my nightdress in the still-packed suitcase. I put my toiletries in the bathroom with its dizzyingly white basin and tiles and turned out the fierce light that made my head throb and went back to bed. I thought about how alone I was and how different I would feel if my husband was with me. He was always good with illness – he often made me bread and sugar in hot milk and fed it to me with a spoon when I was sick. I cried for a while and then sleep claimed me again.

At two in the morning, I woke. I felt terrible, weak as a kitten. My head throbbed and my stomach was rumbling but the thought of food made me nauseous. I took two more painkillers with lots of water. I doubted I could sleep. God knows what time it was in Australia. Probably daytime.

Then I remembered the books I had packed, so I got *Midnight in Sicily* out of my hand luggage and started reading about Sicily, Naples, Rome, the Mafia, Falcone, Borsellino and the other 'distinguished corpses' the Mafia was so proud of. I had a DVD at home called *Five Moons Square* (Donald Sutherland) and it held an eerie fascination for me. I had watched it countless times-and never understood it. When I reached the chapter on the kidnapping of Aldo Moro, that became very clear. Peter Robb's knowledge of Italy was encyclopaedic: the food, the customs, the corruption, the American soldiers who arrived in Italy after World War Two and made the Italian Mafia a branch office of US organised crime. The situation in Palermo was simply that the Mafia was the government. *Midnight in Sicily* is a horror movie. The sixteen-year-old boy who swears to avenge the murder of his father by the Mafia has his right arm hacked off before he is killed. That being the arm he would have used to kill Toto Riina, who had ordered his father's murder. The thirteen-year-old boy who had been kidnapped at eleven and held prisoner by the Mafia for two years, before they murdered him. He offered no resistance, the boy's strangler said in his testimony, 'his strength already being exhausted'. The boy's father had been one of those who laid the explosives that blew up Judge Falcone but he had become an informer. I forgot my aching head, my lightheaded feverishness, the pain beginning in my arms and legs. The hallucinatory evil of the Mafia seemed to be part of my illness. As if the Mafia and I had been bitten by the same rabid dog.

On and on it went: the thirteen-year-old boy who had seen something he shouldn't and who was kidnapped, tied up, blinded and sent home tied up like a salami and 'gushing blood'. Horrible but so beautifully written and so crisply reasoned that it was impossible not to read on, hoping, perhaps, to reach the place where the Mafia was destroyed, because very soon I hated and despised them. They were fond of kidnapping and murdering union leaders too. Being the Fascists they are, organised labour was one of their bête noires. Why did they keep that eleven-year-old boy for two years? Why not just kill him? Was he, like the teenagers in Salo, kept alive so he could be sexually abused?

Waiting for the painkillers to take effect and to ease my aching arms, I put the book down and picked up the news clippings. If I hadn't already been nauseated, the clippings would have done it. Berlusconi: the surreal headline read, 'Berlusconi puts Italy's Judiciary on Trial', accompanied by a photo of the Mafia puppet leaving court in 1996. The 'statute of limitations let him escape charges of corruption, illegal financing of a political party and tax fraud'. There was also a description of how Berlusconi's government had rushed laws through the parliament that partly decriminalised 'false accounting' and shortened the 'time limit on some trials'. Justice had 'gone mad', quoth Berlusconi. Racked as I was with pain, I had to laugh.

At some point, the painkillers must have worked. When I woke again, it was ten a.m. and light was streaming in through the window, hurting my eyes and making my head spin. I picked up the phone and ordered breakfast in my room. Scrambled eggs and coffee. Not because I was hungry but I was now incredibly weak from not eating. I managed to swallow some of the scrambled egg and sipped at the coffee but my stomach revolted at the thought of bread. I hauled myself out of bed and weaved across the floor pushing the trolley and succeeded in putting it out in the hall. When I had to walk back to bed without the trolley, I realised how sick I still was. Back into bed. I opened *Midnight in Sicily* and read on.

And so the week passed. Reading, sleeping, painkillers, showers and room service for meals. I thanked the capricious gods who had done this to me that I had a credit card.

Soon the week was up and I woke on Thursday with a clear head, no pain but still light-headed and a bit wobbly on my feet. By Friday, I told myself I would be able to see Rome! I got out my Lonely Planet guide and started checking out palazzi. There was a map but I had never been any good at reading maps and I didn't intend to start now. That morning, I was able to eat my entire breakfast.

My mobile rang. It was Linda, the single, much-travelled work colleague. 'How's it going? How are you enjoying Rome?'

At the sound of her Australian voice, a single tear ran down my cheek. I wiped it away. 'You won't believe this,' I told her. 'You just won't believe it…'

When I woke Friday morning, I was determined to salvage something from my trip, so I decided to begin with the Museo Napleonica at Piazza di Ponte Umberto 1. I was not up to trains or buses, so I called a cab and went down to wait in front of the hotel. The cab took me to the entrance of the museum. Entry was through an archway with columns. Very grand. And inside was breathtaking beauty: walls in pale blue, pink and plum and everything connected to Napoleon on display. Seemingly endless rooms of the most exquisite bric-a-brac and huge paintings on the walls. Napoleon on a white horse was a popular subject. Paintings of Josephine and Napoleon on a throne. Busts of Napoleon abounded. It was impossible to take it all in but I would probably never get another chance, so I pressed on. I took my time and strolled for about an hour. But after all, I thought, Napoleon was a thug too, in his own way, just like the Mafia. His killers wore uniforms; that was the only difference. It was sad, really, that so much beauty was collected there to honour a man whose real genius was for organising slaughter.

My rumbling stomach finally drove me out in search of food. Online, someone had recommended La Bistroteca as being near the Museo Napoleonica and had raved about the lasagne, so I walked to the Via dell'Orso 71, famished and looking forward to a glass of wine. It was a cosy place with brick walls and pine furniture. I found a table and ordered lasagne and a glass of wine. The food was delicious and I hadn't eaten properly for days so it was like the food of the gods. The wine added a nice rubbery feeling to my legs. I had all day to laze around and as I sat there I thought about the mystery of Italy – a place where people knew how to live so well and yet had allowed a monstrous thing like the Mafia to take root. I studied my guidebook too and decided on the Galleria Nazionale d'Arte Moderna for tomorrow. It had paintings by Klimt, Degas, Cézanne and Monet, Max Ernst and van Gogh, as well as sculpture by Giacometti. Also a bookshop and gift shop. I ordered coffee.

In *Midnight in Sicily*, Peter Robb a caffeine addict and connoisseur, claimed that the only good coffee was in Naples but I was pretty sure that what he would have considered good coffee would appal me – coffee that was black, thick, bitter and that you could stand a spoon up in. I liked my coffee milky, mild and with as little bite as possible. I had ordered a half-strength at La Bistroteca and it was perfect. Here I was again, sleeping in a bedroom in a foreign country, but it was all so different. He wasn't there and he never would be again. This thought put a lump in my throat which I resolutely swallowed with the coffee.

Then, as if on cue, I looked out the door of the restaurant and saw a couple of young lovers across the street, leaning casually on a wall, arms wrapped around each other, kissing playfully. They looked like students – the girl had waist-length hair. Young, young, young. I shook my head slightly as if to clear it and put my eyes back on the tourist guide, started reading about Ostia Antica. I was planning to take a train trip there in a few days. I remembered him kissing me up against a wall in Germany when I was that girl's age. I had also had long black hair, almost to my waist. But that kiss wasn't playful, it was hungry and almost electric. The fire was even in my bones. When I came out into the street and called a cab, the young lovers had vanished, as if they had never existed.

Back at the hotel, I flopped on the bed and went back to *Midnight in Sicily*. The cover illustration was a detail from *Basket of Fruit* by Caravaggio and, true to his code, the fruit, while exquisite, had black spots. Beauty and corruption – like Italy. My goal of finally setting my eyes on some actual Caravaggios would soon be achieved. The Galleria Nazionale d'Arte Antica had *Narcissus*. Unfortunately, *Boy bitten by a Lizard* was in Florence.

When perusing Caravaggio's paintings online on my laptop, I was amused to see that he had even given Medusa his own face. Looking at Medusa, I considered Mafia wives. Peter Robb found them fascinating and despicable, though he didn't put it in those words. What he did say was that divorce was out of the question. A Mafioso can play around as much as he wants but marriage is forever. The wife stays at home; the husband goes out and sells heroin or collects money or rigs up bombs or delivers deadly messages and the wife stays home and does the housework and brings up the children and has a hot meal waiting when father came home after a day of financial crime and a couple of homicides. If you leave out the criminal sadism, it's all a bit like *Leave it to Beaver* or *Father Knows Best* – those lying domestic sitcoms from the fifties. Above all, writes Robb, a Mafia wife goes to Mass and keeps her mouth shut. Don't miss Mass but if, like the journalist Pecorelli, you write an article detailing how Prime Minister Andreotti wrote cheques that proved his involvement with the Mafia, then you will be shot to death in your car. In the chapter on Aldo Moro's kidnapping, Robb also writes that Moro admitted during his interrogation by the Red Brigades that the Christian Democrats were partly funded by the CIA. This can hardly have come as a shock to Moretti, head of the Red Brigades, who was also on the CIA payroll, according to *Five Moons Square*.

Next day, I caught a tram to the Galleria Nazionale d'Arte Moderna. The place is a 'vast belle époque palace' according to Lonely Planet and the art runs from neoclassical romantic sculpture to abstract expressionist paintings. I would be wandering lonely as a cloud except that I wasn't lonely. There was only one person I wanted to share all of this with and he was gone. Gone into what Che Guevara once called 'the mystery that surrounds us all'. And gets us all in the end, he could have added, I told myself bitterly.

Rattling along on the tram, I studied an art book I had packed, and became fixated on Caravaggio among the constellation of art stars on display. Born Michelangelo Merisi in 1571, he killed a man in a brawl and fled Rome. Died not long after on 18 July 1610. When Caravaggio was six, bubonic plague killed almost everyone in his family, including his father. His fatal flaw stemmed from this catastrophe, some have said, as if he carried some kind of survivor guilt and was bound to pluck failure from the jaws of victory. As an orphan, he was free to roam the streets and took up with a group of painters and swordsmen who took as their motto, *nec spe, nec metu*, 'without hope, without fear'. This is what I see in his paintings – that darkness. Nihilism before anyone even knew what it was. He did not do worshipful paintings of saints and his *St Matthew and the Angel* caused such an uproar he had to redo it. The man he killed was a Roman pimp called Ranuccio Tomassoni. Tempting to see it as a good deed, although some say the cause of the fight was Caravaggio's lust for Tomassoni's wife, Lavinia. Even when he painted Jesus rising from the dead (*Resurrection*), he shows an untidy Jesus fleeing his tomb in the middle of the night, as if he had not paid his rent. But the scandals were only of their time. In Rome in 2010, an exhibition of his work marking the four hundredth anniversary of his death drew more than 580,000 visitors. With all his flaws, people know he is one of us, as they do van Gogh – a modern ahead of his time.

I almost missed my stop, deep in thoughts of Caravaggio. There were more majestic pillars at the entrance and colourful banners hanging between them. In one vast room, large, colourful toy grubs lay on the floor like abandoned toys. I stopped further on before a painting by Plinio Nomellini, *Bambine sui Mare*, showing two beautiful children wading in the ocean. Lots of pinks and blues and perfect skin tones. But I was in search of stronger stuff and had to will myself not to look at everything. Soon I saw a van Gogh – *The Gardener* 1889. Then there was a Klimt. I drank it all in. I spotted a Degas, a nude woman drying herself after her bath. A burst of scarlet, Max Ernst. Another van Gogh, *L'Arlesienne*.

I wandered on in a happy daze. After a while, I needed a rest and I saw they had provided couches for this purpose. I took a breather but while I sat there all I could think about was the Galleria Nazionale d'Arte

Antica and the feast that awaited me. I was a glutton for art. Soon I was standing in front of some Monet water lilies. Deeply moved by them and soothed in some way. The crazy swirls of Jackson Pollock snapped me back to the present. Then I stopped stock-still in front of a sculpture. A girl's perfect, barely pubescent body, dragonfly wings on her back. I stood there for some time entranced by perfection.

This went on for hours until I was too tired to walk any more. Back on the tram to the hotel, I almost fell asleep.

In the following days, I took the train trip to Ostia Antica for the frescoes and murals. I even visited the Museo Leonardo da Vinci and studied his incredible inventions, products of the same genius that produced his art. But I considered the highlight of my trip would be the Galleria Nazionale d'Arte Antica and Caravaggio. I consulted Lonely Planet. The Antica was in the Palazzo Orsini/Barberini, once home to Queen Christina of Sweden: her richly frescoed bedroom witnessed a steady stream of male and female lovers. One of the highlights of the Antica, according to Lonely Planet was *San Giovanni Battista* (John the Baptist) by Caravaggio. I travelled to the gallery on the 870 bus from Piazza delle Rovere. The area where the Antica stood, Trastevere, was once working-class and poor but is now chic and pricey so I had scoured LP for the best value restaurant. Panettoni at Viale di Trastevere 53 sounded right.

The palazzo was a huge, pale building, elegant and graceful. My heart actually skipped a beat as I entered the grounds. I could feel it hammering away in my chest. I went through decorated stone posts and metal gates to reach the building. Soon I was standing in front of a beautiful sculpture, lit from above – so white and ethereal it seemed it could float away. A kind of trinity. A woman centre top with two winged angels on either side. On a lower level, two rearing horses and lower still a face; it seemed to be male but I had no idea what it was meant to represent. No sculpture, I told myself, you're here for the paintings – especially Caravaggio. So I pressed on, averting my gaze from the sculptures. I stopped in front of an 'El Descendimiento', Christ's body being lowered from the cross, and it is very long, very white and he looks very dead.

I keep walking and suddenly I'm in another large room with pink walls and I'm looking at *Narcissus* on the wall. Genius, I think. No other word. The perfect rendering of human frailty (and who knew more about that than Caravaggio?) leaps out at me. Beautiful Narcissus in his silky blue and white clothes entranced and doomed leaning over to gaze at himself in water as dark and still as a jewel, his reflection indistinct. The look of tenderness he gives his reflection is perfect and tragic, as it should be, given his fate. I would love to have studied *Young Sick Bacchus* the same way but it was in the Galleria Borghese. Of course, inevitably, I thought of the thirteen-year-old boy strangled by the Mafia. He had not struggled; his strength was spent. Was he ill? Had two years of imprisonment and possibly sexual abuse broken his spirit? No doubt it had and he may have resembled Caravaggio's Bacchus.

I pushed these horrible thoughts away but the next painting of Caravaggio's showed St Francis meditating on a human skull, which did nothing to alleviate my gloom. Where was the 'luminous' *Giovanni Battista* to lift my spirits? But when I find it, he is a skinny youth, half naked sitting in the dark and over his shoulder I think I can make out the face of an animal which could also be a demon or even the Devil himself. Is it actually there? It seems to be. Was it the demon that looked over Caravaggio's shoulder for his entire, shockingly short life? This is a vulnerable John the Baptist, a vulnerable boy and perhaps he resembles the young boy the Mafia blinded and sent home gushing blood, according to *Midnight in Sicily*.

I need sunlight. I feel as if Caravaggio's darkness is choking me. I find a side door and make a hasty exit. Even genius can make you despair. Perhaps especially genius. I think of Goya and his painting of Saturn devouring his son.

Lonely Planet had told me that Panettoni is nicknamed 'L'Obitorio' (the morgue) because of its marble-topped tables. But I feast on delicious thin-crust pizza after an entrée of risotto balls and a glass of white wine, and I don't mind the marble. My spirits revive and I catch a bus back to the hotel. I haven't cooked a single meal in the lovely kitchen at the hotel and I feel lazy but, after all, I'm on holiday, so room service it is.

As I got off the bus, a kind young man with a beautiful smile helped me down to the pavement. Then he tried to steal my handbag but I fought with all my strength, the straps broke and he fell backwards and then fled, seeming to vanish into thin air. With two days to go, I had no intention of losing my ID and credit cards. Feeling rattled, I made my way into the hotel room and sat at the kitchen table, noticing suddenly that my legs were trembling. So now I needed another handbag and I would go out tomorrow, hit the shops near the Spanish Steps and get one. He probably thought I was an easy target, I told myself, putting the kettle on for a restorative coffee.

I spend the last couple of days lazing around and reading. I had found a bookshop near the Spanish Steps and bought two (expensive) books on Rome as well as a red handbag. I had a feeling I would come back to Rome.

It's only when I'm in the plane looking down on the city as it flies away from the plane that I realise I got it wrong in 1980. The Coliseum was only one face of Rome. There were actually three: the brutal, imperial face of Ancient Rome, typified by the Coliseum and what went on there; the beautiful, untruthful face of the art, the buildings, the grandeur, paid for by the Roman Empire or the Catholic Church; and lastly, the monstrously cruel and evil face of the crime and corruption controlled by the Mafia. At twenty-two, I had only seen the first face. The three faces are relentless, pitiless and completely Italian, a product of its history. Beautiful as it was, the art was like the painted face of a whore, disguising the cold, calculating cruelty of the church that paid for it. That is partly what made Caravaggio respond in kind. Murdered on a beach, dying a murderer himself. The devil may have guided his knife but angels guided his brush. His life was short and brutal but fortunately the saying held true: 'Life is short, art is long.'

For the second time in my life, I watched Rome recede, with no regrets.

A Delirium

I was newly divorced. I blame it on that. I was vulnerable. Vulnerable enough to go on an online dating site. He was handsome, had a lovely smile. I could hardly believe my luck. We arranged to meet. It was one of those sites where the woman has to make contact. He had a deep, sexy voice on the phone. How could he look as good as his photo? He did. A silver fox with ice blue eyes and one of those expensive tans. I felt like a cliché as I gazed into his eyes and felt swept away before he had so much as spoken. He walked in and the earth moved, not in a circle but sideways.

'Hi,' he said with a million-candlepower smile. 'I'm Greg and you must be Karen.' He laughed but in the long run the joke was on me.

We were in a fancy coffee shop with white tablecloths and wait staff who looked like models.

He sat down, keeping his eyes on my face and a burst of heat rose up from my breasts and flamed up my neck and face. I felt panic nibbling at my toes. Could I handle this? Could I handle him? I was feeling as flighty as a schoolgirl. I had no idea, no idea at all, why I was so worried and so wary. It was my spidey senses warning me but I was in no mood to listen.

First time in bed was so sensational I wrote it up in my diary.

> Had sex. Came. Lovely. He's so passionate. He talks in his sleep but I couldn't understand a word. He has a perfect body and he's over six feet tall. Yum.

There were lots of entries like that.

Had sex and it didn't take long to come. I would have liked it to last longer, but I can't have everything!

Had sex. I wanted it pretty badly so it didn't take long to come. He went to sleep after and I gazed adoringly at him while a beautiful cool breeze blew in the window and touched my skin.

Had sex. He made me get on top. It was yummy and I stuck my breast in his mouth. Orgasm was extended. I'm throbbing just thinking about it.

Had sex. Long, hot, sweaty…

And so on.

I worried that it was 'only sex' even though he took me out every Friday night and stayed until Sunday night, just like a real boyfriend. I obsessed that I wasn't showing him enough affection in bed. I ran my hands all over him and kissed his body. At one point I recorded in my diary that I wanted to suck and kiss his nipples but hadn't dared at that point. When I did suck his nipples (finally), I asked him, 'Do you feel anything when I do that?'

'No,' he said laughing. 'I'm not a woman.'

I had his erect penis in my hand at the time, so that was more than obvious.

He was easy-going, calm but passionate in bed. I was in heaven. Had I found the perfect man? Better late than never. I was given a post-coital treat once when he thought he might have torn some skin under his foreskin (he wasn't circumcised) as he worked hard to give me an orgasm. His took his glistening, still-erect penis in his hand and pulled the foreskin back to check for damage. Lots of shiny pinks and purples to view as I lay there sweating and post-orgasmic.

Sometimes when he came strongly, I could feel him pumping semen into me and I would think, 'How can heaven be better than this?' Afterwards, I asked myself absurdly, 'Is that sacrilege?'

Soon after that, the trouble started. Out to dinner in some glamorous restaurant, he would seem distracted when I spoke to him.

'What?' he would say with that brilliant smile and I would repeat what I had said.

Then one night he simply didn't show up. Calls to his mobile phone weren't answered. Texts weren't answered either. I didn't sleep all night, convinced that he was dead or, much worse, that he was ghosting me and I would never hear from him again. It was over, I told myself. The thought was like a knife inside me, tearing at my vitals. But surely he couldn't be that cruel? Little did I know.

He came back a week later. There had been a car accident. Nothing serious but he hadn't wanted to worry me. I pointed out that I had been worried. He put his arms around me and I melted against him the way I always did. I noticed that his car didn't have a scratch on it but he said he had already been to the panel beater. Perfectly credible. His car was his baby. He had told me that more than once. A shiny red Mazda X5. I loved his car and loved it when he drove me around in it. He told me he was a lawyer in a busy inner-city practice, which was why he couldn't see me through the week. Again, perfectly credible.

What would I do if I lost him? It was like thinking about dying. Usually on Saturday mornings, he would go out and buy the papers, crispy bread rolls and chocolate. Then we would have sex and afterwards he would make coffee to have with the bread rolls. Then we would read the papers in bed while eating chocolate. Then we would have sex again.

I couldn't pretend any longer. I told him I loved him.

He looked startled: not the reaction I was expecting or hoping for.

'Princess,' – he always called me princess – 'let's not rush things.'

'I don't want to rush things,' I said, 'but I love you and I wanted to say it.'

His eyes were usually blue but sometimes they went grey. They were grey now. 'Princess, you're such a sweetie,' he crooned, 'but I've been burned. I want to take it slowly.'

He didn't say he loved me. In fact, he never did. So he was honest about that at least.

Propped up on the pillows, looking so handsome, he told me that he was going to a conference in Paris. My heart leapt. Paris! But wives and girlfriends weren't allowed. He would be going alone. I swallowed my disappointment and soon after was bouncing up and down on his penis while he kissed my mouth and my throat.

It would be months before I knew the truth about the 'conference'. He was actually at the beach with a woman at that time. He confessed when things were getting rocky. Throwing me a truth that covered up a much bigger lie.

When he got back from 'Paris', even though he was 'jetlagged', he wanted to go to bed and he was tender and sweet and I loved him even more. I felt lucky and I went on feeling lucky until a blonde turned up at my door one day looking for Greg.

'He's not here,' I told her. 'He doesn't live here. He's only here at the weekend.'

'He said he'd call me. I followed him Friday night and he came here. He hasn't called.'

I felt myself go cold. It started in my feet and spread slowly upwards until it reached the top of my head.

'Are you all right?' said the blonde. 'You look pale.'

'He's with me now,' I told her. 'He's my boyfriend.'

She looked scornful. 'I don't think he's anyone's boyfriend. He has a lot of women, I know that, I think he could be married too, but I'm in love with him.' She began to cry.

I tried to speak but found I couldn't. After a while, she went away.

He was contrite when I phoned him.

'I'm so sorry, princess. She's stalking me. She just can't let go. I broke up with her months ago but she won't accept it.'

He probably said all this while he was in a hotel room with yet another woman. Later, much later, I pictured her in the shower unable to hear anything he was saying. I decided she would have been blonde. By then, I knew he preferred blondes. I was a brunette.

'I should have warned you,' he was saying. 'She tracks me wherever I go. I'm starting to think she has a tracking device on my phone.' He laughed. A lot.

I realised I'd been holding my breath, so I exhaled. 'Oh,' I said. 'Oh, babe, that's terrible. Have you told the police?'

'There's nothing they can do. They're useless for things like this,' he said. 'I'll be over later,' he added.

And he was as good as his word. A couple of hours later, he turned up sporting a sheepish grin, looking edible in a black muscle shirt and tight white pants. Work had been full on, he told me. Now, I think he had spent the night screwing another woman. He told me with a delicious grin that he didn't know if he could rise to the occasion. I knew how to fix that. I straddled him, kissed his body and squeezed his penis until it was hard, guided his penis in, put a breast in his mouth, had an orgasm. Then I fell on my back, guided him in again, flexed my pelvic muscles, while holding his gorgeous butt in my hands and made him come. Did he have any idea how lucky he was? No, he didn't. I don't think he even believed in luck. He believed he deserved it. Things just came to him. They always had. The saying 'The beautiful make their own rules' applied to him and he believed that was perfectly just. His reaction to sexual pleasure was that he always wanted more and with as many women as possible. He deserved that, too.

As women tend to do with this kind of man, I believed him. I believed he was being stalked by the blonde; it was kind of true but not anything like the truth. Almost everything he told me was in the same category. His mother was not a doctor, she was a nurse. His father was not an architect, he was a builder. He didn't have two siblings, he was an only child. He was not a wealthy businessman, he was a bankrupt businessman. I was like someone with a fever: deliriously in love with someone who didn't exist. Even when I was alone, I would lie in bed thinking about what I would do to him next time we were having sex. Thinking about his body, his smile, his voice, his laugh. I was easy to fool. I confided to my diary that I was insatiable. That however much we had sex, it would never be enough. I had turned into a teenage boy. I believed I loved him. I felt sure we would end up married. On that front, I was a teenage girl. He had no such intentions. He wasn't going to deny his gifts in bed to any woman. I regarded him as honest, decent and kind. He was none of those things.

He came to see me less and less. Soon I was writing in my diary, 'Mad for sex.'

When he finally turned up, I would eat him alive.

Once after sex, he said to me with his dazzling smile, 'I think one day all they'll find is my bones.'

I was bathed in sweat and drifting in post-orgasmic glow at the time. I kissed his chest, his hands, his belly. I licked his nipples. I kissed his penis.

He laughed and said, 'My sweet little pussy.'

And that's exactly what I was to him. Pussy. Then I went to sleep. When I woke, he was gone. I didn't panic. He was mysterious like that.

About a week later, he was back and spent the night. We had sex twice but, of course, however many times we had it would never be enough. It was damn nice, though.

Around three in the morning, he kissed me passionately and asked me. 'Are you happy?'

Happy? I was satisfied, certainly, but happy? I knew something was wrong and the wariness I felt when I first met him was now more insistent. But I lied and said I was happy.

He said softly, 'My princess is happy. What more can I ask for?' and kissed my breasts.

When I woke around eight a.m., he was gone again.

The truth was there all the time. All I had to do was google his name but I didn't do that until after I already knew the truth.

One lovely spring day, I was sitting at the outdoor table of a coffee shop sipping a cappuccino under a pretty pink umbrella with the Cat's Pyjamas written on it – the brand of coffee they used. The coffee shop was called Ultrablue. It was my favourite. The whole place was a shimmering light blue, like a haze rising off the sea, except for the pink umbrellas. The waitresses wore black shorts and white shirts, so did the waiters. They were all so good-looking I thought they must be actors or acting students waiting to be discovered. And there he suddenly was, on the other side of the road, holding hands with a beautiful blonde woman. Following them, like ducklings, was a bevy of blonde beauties (four of them). Their children, all girls. Man and wife were talking and looking at each other. They didn't see me.

I knew my mouth was, ridiculously, hanging open but I couldn't seem to close it. I reached out, for what I don't know, and knocked my coffee cup over, spilling coffee all over the table. Dreading I would attract attention and he would see me, I quickly mopped it up with serviettes and then rushed into the coffee shop and stayed there until they had walked off up the road. The sun streaming in the window dazzled me and made me feel sick. Little black dots that seemed to have feathered edges danced before my eyes. I thought I was having some kind of breakdown so I fled the coffee shop and went home. I had planned to check out a new art gallery two blocks from the coffee shop but that was now impossible. My legs could barely support me.

Driving home, my mind raced. What if there were other children, other wives? It wasn't impossible at all. With someone like him, anything was possible. I could see that now. Everything I thought I knew was gone, vaporised. Of course she could be his sister but the way he was looking at her ruled that out. He was holding her hand too, not normal brotherly behaviour. Did they have an arrangement? Did she know?

Inevitably, he turned up at my place again. He was tanned. His eyes glinted like blue diamonds. He was sexy and sweet – the way he always was – and I was so far gone I almost convinced myself there was some logical explanation other than the truth for what I had seen. I was so greedy for him I decided I would tell him the jig was up after we had sex. And we did. All night.

The thought of his wife and the blonde ducklings never came near me while I lay with him skin to skin and loved him in an uncomplicated way. But it could never be uncomplicated now. For the first time, I understood why women accepted an arrangement, made a deal and shared their man. But I knew I could never do that.

The next morning, it rained. I was sad and tired. He was full of beans. He was one of those people who woke, his feet hit the floor and he was on, as if a switch had been thrown. He was an actor who never stopped acting. All his personas were juggled with astonishing skill and callous disregard for the truth and those he hurt. I couldn't help crying. I knew what I had to do and it was breaking my heart.

'I saw you with your wife and kids,' I told him, as tears poured down my face.

He never missed a beat. 'We're divorced,' he said and put his arms around me.

I wanted to believe him but I knew it was a lie. 'I suppose she's got money,' I said, blowing my nose.

That stopped him in his tracks. How the hell does she know that? His face was a question mark.

'Makes sense. That's why you have the time to chase women. You don't work, do you? You don't need to. What's the family business?'

Now he knew it was hopeless. I had figured it out. Figured him out.

'Her father owns a chain of hardware stores,' he said, staring into space. 'There are shares and real estate investments. She's wealthy, yes, you're right.' He was silent for a while. Then he said, 'It wasn't just sex. With you, I mean.'

Like everything else he ever said to me, it was true enough but nowhere near the truth.

I had an epiphany. 'It was for me,' I said. 'You're the best I ever had. You're like a drug.'

He smiled, uncertainly. I almost expected him to say thank you but he didn't. Then I cried my eyes out. I couldn't stop. It was all too messy for him. He walked away from me to the bathroom and took a shower. Washing me off him. Moving on.

When he came out again, clean and beautiful, he couldn't meet my eyes. He picked up his watch and his car keys from the bedside table, bent down to kiss me but I turned my head.

'Don't,' I said.

I listened to his car drive away, dried my eyes and called a friend. 'Come over,' I told her. 'I have to get out of the house tonight or I'll top myself.'

'Christ, what happened?'

'I'll tell you, but not now.'

I wiggled into a slinky black dress, did my face, put on too-high shoes and a silver necklace my mother had given me. I knew I would have a hangover in the morning. I might even stay up all night. There was a pain I couldn't place. It wasn't in my heart. I hurt all over. I went to the kitchen in my glad rags and waited for my friend, sipping Chardonnay.

It was still raining. I could hear the rain outside. Steady and constant. A way he would never be.

The Pointy End

Ordinary day. Beautiful day. Spring. I woke up and I felt great. It was Monday and some people don't like Mondays, but I had no bias that way. I may have liked Friday more because it was the end of the working week but I didn't mind my job, so Monday was not a bad day in my mind.

All that changed when I walked up the lane next to the finance company where I worked and went in the back door as I always did. Ordinary day. Until I looked at the walls of the 'recreation room', where the car dealers came to be entertained by the credit managers. I felt dizzy. I was stunned and angry and I shouted, 'What the hell?' The day had changed from ordinary to bizarre.

On the previous Friday, while we were at home cooking dinner, the car dealers had come to meet the manager of personal loans for booze and to play games in the recreation room. One of the games they played was billiards; there was a billiards table and a bar. The other game they played was there for all to see, all over the walls. There were large black and white photos of naked women with darts sticking out of them. They had obviously won points for which body part they hit, with the highest points being reserved, of course, for a direct hit on the vagina.

Soon, other women arrived for work. Usually there was chatter but the sight of the photos and the darts caused an unnatural silence. We stood around. Silently. We were ashamed. Not of the men who had done this – we were ashamed we were female.

We knew we had to do something but had no idea what that might be. I had not yet read *The Second Sex* or *The Female Eunuch*. None of us had. But we knew this was wrong. Even our unraised consciousness rebelled. After some discussion, we decided we had to go to the manager and complain. He was a sexist, of course; they all were – it was the seventies.

The manager was involved in a hot and heavy affair with the married Robin. His wife was pregnant with their third child and Robin's husband seemed like a bit of a lowlife to me. He wore moleskins, which was fine, but he also wore a cowboy hat. Even indoors. I didn't like him, but still. My sympathies were with the manager's wife, not Robin. It all came out eventually and Robin married her manager but at the time they were both in a bad situation. Robin refused to get involved in our resistance, for obvious reasons. Only five of us decided it was not to be endured.

'It's enough to make you vomit,' said Carmel, red-haired, overwrought and married.

'How can they be such animals?' raged Sandra, plain, skinny and married.

'Why would they do such a thing?' wondered Carol, tiny, blonde, pretty and married to a policeman.

'Revolting!' sneered Leah, tall, goddessy-looking with long black hair and very red lips. She was a loose woman but married.

I was married too. Only one female in the office was not. A blonde typist.

We agreed that we had to go to the manager and complain. We needed a leader and I was forced into the role. No one else wanted to lead the rebellion. I agreed reluctantly but if I'd known the reputation it would give me, I think I might have decided it was a bad idea. I was always going to be seen as a ballbreaker and a feminist bitch ever after. Even though I wasn't a feminist. I didn't know enough then to be one, but I knew what I didn't like. So we formed our band of resisters and walked warily to Mike Monroe's office.

Mike was a tall, handsome man with curly blond hair and shrewd blue eyes. Late thirties. He oozed sex appeal. He looked startled when we filed into his office. Was it someone's birthday? Would he have to sign a card? 'Ladies,' he said, with a cheerful smile.

'I have to talk to you about something,' I told him.

'It's horrible,' said Carol, and Monroe sat forward expectantly.

'When we arrived for work this morning, there were photos of naked women all over the walls of the recreation room with darts sticking out of them,' I blurted out.

'Darts?' He gave me a look that made me think he thought I was pulling his leg.

'Yes, darts,' I confirmed. 'We don't expect to be confronted with this…'

'Filth,' Carmel said.

But, of course, it wasn't the nudity. It was the violence, the hatred, the contempt. We barely understood it, so we didn't put it into words.

Monroe rose to his full height – about six foot two, I estimated – and said, 'Show me.'

We did.

He stood there amazed and angry.

'How can they be so stupid?' he said, and I realised he meant, how could they be stupid enough to leave them there?

It wasn't what I wanted him to say but at least he was angry. Not angry the right way, but angry.

'Don't worry,' Monroe said. 'I'll deal with this.'

We thanked him and returned to our desks. Then we saw the manager from personal loans, a snotty little bastard I had always disliked (now I knew why), heading up to Monroe's office. He ambled by with not a care in the world and we traded glances and snickered. He had shiny black hair cut close to his head, like a helmet. He walked with the lanky, boneless walk of a teenage boy in a growth spurt and was as good-looking as a pop star. (Irish genes.} His attitude to women obviously matched his looks. We were excited but scared the way do-gooders always are when they take on the beast of wrong and indeed evil. I wanted good to triumph over evil. I always did. I was a goody two shoes as a child and I hadn't changed. We trusted Monroe to do right, which, considering he was a sexist and an adulterer, was naïve in the extreme.

This was an era when I read magazines and was into fashion in a big way. It wasn't until much later that I read books like *The Feminist Papers, Essays on Sex Equality, The Rights and Wrongs of Women, Women's Estate, S.C.U.M. Manifesto*. I went through a real feminist awakening about ten years later and it's more than likely that the memory of those photos with darts sticking out of them put me on that path. If I had known the things in those books in the seventies, my response to what those men had done would have been far more militant. I wasn't even capable of thinking, 'Imagine if those photos had been of naked Jews or naked blacks.' I hadn't read *Sexual Politics*, in which Kate Millett refers to the fact that Marx believed that the first coloniszation is always of women. I didn't understand the nature of fascism either. Nor did I understand that from the Bible to Darwin to Freud, the male is presented as the true human and the female is presented as an inferior human. It's that which allows men to rationalise raping, beating and murdering women for being failed men, for being subhuman. Looking at those photos, I only knew that it was wrong, that it came from contempt and hatred and illustrated a desire to degrade women and to hurt them. The dart was a phallic symbol but I knew nothing much about them either. That being the case, it's ironic I was tagged as a mad feminist and a man-hater from that day forward.

Marx believed that without the colonisation of women, all the other injustices – including racism and the class system – could never have come about. For white men to be superior, black men have to be inferior. For all men to be superior, all women have to be inferior. My mind didn't work this way in the seventies. It barely worked at all, I realise now. Still, my response to the photos and the men who threw the darts was visceral. A group apology to every woman in the office was required.

Aristotle described 'woman' as an impotent male. I was about to learn why. We were right in our outrage and desire for an apology. We were sure of that. So we waited for right to be rewarded and wrong to be defeated. As we waited, forces we had not considered were gathering and their aim was to move some portion of blame on to the resisters and to remove the stigma of sexism, crudeness, sadism and poor taste from themselves.

In the end, what the manager of personal loans came up with was pure genius. I had always known he was a clever little shit and he was about to prove it. Nietzsche, in *Thus Spake Zarathustra*, referred to the healthy selfishness that comes from a powerful soul. The little shit was the epitome of a powerful soul and he was clever, very clever. We sat at our desks and did our work. The little shit walked back and forth between his office and Mike Monroe's office. Many times. Negotiations were under way.

Monroe demanded an apology, as we later discovered. All that remained to be settled was what form the apology would take. That proved to be the pointy end, as pointy as the end of those darts. We watched personal loans walk backwards and forwards to Monroe's office and giggled foolishly. Monroe was dragging him over the coals and we loved it. We didn't know what form the apology would take but an apology would be a victory, so that was a good thing. So we thought.

By three p.m., the message came that the five resisters and their leader (me) were to go to Mike Monroe's office. We filed in somewhat sheepishly and Mike greeted us with a broad smile. He had fought the good fight and won.

He was beaming. 'Well,' he said, leaning forward. 'We've reached a compromise.'

'That's great,' I said, and the others nodded.

'Barry' – that was the little shit's name – 'has agreed to apologise.'

'Wonderful,' I said, beaming myself now.

'But he will only apologise to Kirsten, because she's not married.'

My jaw literally dropped. 'Not married?' I babbled. 'What…does…that…mean?' I stammered. 'What does that have to do with it?'

'Well, he's adamant. He feels the married women shouldn't have been so shocked. They know what men are like.'

Shouldn't have been so shocked? 'I don't understand,' I said.

'Well, that's his position. That is the only way he'll apologise,' Monroe said. Apologetically. 'I've asked him to reconsider several times, but that is his position,' he added with an air of finality, and we knew the discussion was over.

At four-thirty, we saw Barry amble over to Kirsten and offer his sham apology. She simpered. She always did around men. She was about twenty-one, blonde, blue eyes, strikingly pretty with lush lips, pneumatic boobs and long tanned legs. He was only too happy to apologise to her but not to us boilers. I saw the way he looked at her and it hit me. They were also having an affair. His 'apology' would earn him brownie points and extra fun in bed. We, the married also-rans, were not worth a minute of his time. He shot us a smug grin as he walked back to his office. And that was that.

'Did you see that grin on his face? The shit,' Leah snarled.

We milled around, looked embarrassed and went back to our desks. We never mentioned the photos or the darts again and if ever the little shit passed our desks after this, it was with the bouncing, victorious stroll of a man returning from a brothel where he had enjoyed several women as if they were chocolates in a foil-wrapped box. We hated him and mocked his helmet of black hair, even speculating that it was a toupee, and suggested he had a tiny, little cock, but he had won. We knew it and so did he. The fact that his wife divorced him six months later wasn't really a defeat for him, because he married Kirsten the following year. They had an enormous wedding at St David's cathedral and we phoned each other and cackled like witches.

'That arsehole,' we cried. 'And that bitch. That huge-titted bitch!'

Things like this made me a feminist but not the other members of the rebellion. Years later, they would still sneer at feminists and when we went to see the feminist film *The Piano*, they hated Ada and said she was a slut because she was unfaithful to her 'husband' even though they were not even married. They didn't understand it at all but I understood it only too well. I cried furtively and was silent as they attacked Ada. I knew it was better to let sleeping dogs lie.

I remembered the day I left the finance company and how they couldn't find anyone among the managers to make a farewell speech and give me my gift and card. Finally, Bob, one of the youngest, who hadn't been there when the dart debacle took place, was pressed into service. I endured it, because I had to, knowing that the label of 'feminist' would not follow me to my new job in another town. 'The Battle of the Darts' hadn't left a mark on Barry but the loss left me labelled a bitch and a troublemaker. I learned to be silent and to obey, hating myself for it.

But I had to thank the little shit for one thing. My skirmish with him showed me the score better than any university degree ever could. There was no romance in it but it was the truth and had its own beauty. Brutal but necessary, like a surgeon's scalpel slicing flesh.

About the Author

Antonia Hildebrand is a poet, short story writer and essayist. She was born and educated in Toowoomba, Queensland. She married Reinhard Hildebrand in the early seventies and moved with him to Hamburg, Germany. She lived and worked in Europe for three years and also travelled in Europe and Asia before returning to Australia. She then studied at the Toowoomba Technical College, going to evening classes before gaining admission to the University of Queensland and graduating Bachelor of Arts in 1987 with a major in English literature. In 1993 she graduated Master of Letters (German) from the University of New England. Her first published short story, 'Nothing Ever Happens', appeared in *Woman's Day* in 1981 and *Downs Images* in 1982 and she has since been widely published in journals, magazines and anthologies in Australia as well as Britain and the USA. Her poems have appeared in *Coppertales, Iodine Poetry Journal, Poetrix, Harvester* and *Squidink*. From 2000 to 2002 she was a member of Crime Writers Queensland and had two stories published in their books – 'The Weeping Madonna' in *Menace in the Mulga* and 'Second Nature' in *Bad to the Bones*. Her short stories have appeared in *Downs Images, Woman's Day, Shortz, First Edition Magazine, Tirra Lirra* and *Four W Seventeen*. An essay on John Howard, 'Ordinary Australians', was published in *Overland* in 2003.

In 1998 she won the University of Southern Queensland Library Poetry Prize and in 1999 the Fellowship of Australian Writers' Marjorie Barnard Short Story Award. In 2002 she began contributing to Radio National's *Bush Telegraph* program. Many of her short stories have been broadcast by *Queensland Storyteller* on Radio 4RPH and by *Words and Music* on Radio 91.3 FM. Her Radio National pieces and her film reviews and essays were collected for her book *The Past is Another Country: Viewpoints, Essays & Reviews* published in 2003. She has also explored growing to adulthood, living in Europe and returning to Australia in the years 1951 to 1975 in her memoir *Beautiful Life*. In 2004 she co-wrote, with John Boshammer, *Boshy and Me*, a biography of his rugby legend father, Kev Boshammer. A poetry collection, *The Sweet Time*, was published in 2006. Other publications include *The Blind Colossus*, an essay collection, 2015; *To Breathe and Other Stories*, 2016; and *War Stories*, a poetry collection, 2017. She was elected president of the Fellowship of Australian Writers Queensland (2015–2016).

Lightning Source UK Ltd.
Milton Keynes UK
UKHW010737150822
407319UK00001B/310